takeover

takeover

a novel

by

RICHARD W. GOFFMAN

99%BOOKS
New York City ◆ Sussex, NJ

ISBN-10: 0-692-69343-2
ISBN-13: 978-0-692-69343-8

PRINTED IN THE UNITED STATES OF AMERICA

Brief excerpts from the following copyrighted works appear in this book for the purpose of providing contemporaneous context. All lyrics and other quotations are property and copyright of their owners.

[1] Pages 55, 198, from "Don't Fear the Reaper" ©1976 by Buck Dharma, Blue Öyster Cult, lyric © SONY/ATV MUSIC PUBLISHING LLC
[2] Page 90, from "Big Yellow Taxi" ©1969 by Joni Mitchell, lyric © Siquomb Publishing Company
[3] Pages 127, 131, 133, from "Sultans of Swing" ©1978 by Dire Straits, written by Mark Knopfler © 1978 Straitjacket Songs Ltd.
[4] Page 136, from "Le Freak" by Chic © 1978 Written by Nile Rodgers, Bernard Edwards, Lyrics © Sony/ATV Music Publishing LLC, Warner/Chappell Music, Inc.
[5] Page 145, 147, from "Stayin' Alive" by The Bee Gees, written by Maurice Ernest Gibb, Robin Hugh Gibb, Barry Alan Gibb Lyrics © 1978 Lyrics © EMI Music Publishing, Sony/ATV Music Publishing LLC, Warner/Chappell Music, Inc., Universal Music Publishing Group.
[6] Page 184, from "I'll Be There For You" by The Rembrandts, written by Michael Jay Skloff, David L. Crane, Marta Fran Kauffman, Allee Willis, Philip Ronald Solem, Danny C. Wilde. Lyrics © 1995 Universal Music Publishing Group
[7] Page 208, from "Finale in the Valley" Lyrics © 99%BOOKS. This Bruce Springsteen and the E Street Band song is not an actual Bruce Springsteen and the E Street Band song. It's a fake. The author of this book wrote it. *Mea culpa.* Having said that, Bruce, if you're interested, call me.

Dedication

Takeover is dedicated to
Dr. Linda Frances Watkins-Goffman
whose exceptional artistic talents and human qualities
are far too numerous to mention in this finite space;
whose brilliance is unquestioned;
and whose inspiration and generosity are
the *sine qua non* for any decent work I ever do.

Thanks

Appreciation must be given to every person
who read some or all of this book
at various stages during its process of becoming itself.
These include: Amy D'Annibale, Diana Flanagan, Susanna Lee,
Linda Watkins-Goffman, and Bill Higbie (Inkus Emeritus),
collectively known as The Inklings, as well as
Bruce Apar, Steven Lam and Anne Sherber.
Thanks also to Steve Leibowitz, who is waiting for the movie.

Birth Announcement

For such a slender book, *Takeover* has had a lengthy gestation.
The first draft was written in November 2001, under the
auspices of National Novel Writing Month
(www.NaNoWriMo.org) and was granted that
organization's highest award.
It sat patiently in a drawer for fourteen years until it rattled its
own cage so loudly that it could not be ignored. At that point I
dusted it off, rewrote it, and let it out into the light of day.

Also by Richard W. Goffman

Heartless Cruelty (2012)
Laid So Low (2015)

Critical Praise for the
Mr. Bachman Series of Jersey Shore Thrillers

HEARTLESS CRUELTY

"If you're looking for the next great suspense novel, look no further than HEARTLESS CRUELTY. Goffman's moody setting, wonderful characters and masterful plotting will have you turning pages late into the night…"

Maryann McFadden, Indie Award-Winning
Novelist of *The Book Lover*

"…to see a writer's mind at work twisting ideas, tricking and surprising us… is an extraordinary thing, a lesson in plot that all writers should pay close attention to. It's exciting to see where and how his mind goes. Cinematic… It has a Dennis Lehane quality about it."

Joe Vallese, Author/Editor of *What's Your Exit?*
A Literary Detour through New Jersey

"…by turns poetic and earthy, shades of Elmore Leonard… Certainly a page turner."

Betsy Hays Gatti, author of *Riding with the Wind*

"It's a great thriller. I couldn't put it down from the time I picked it up. Exciting story, great writing. I can't wait for the next one.

Detective Sgt. (ret) Pablo Maute,
Paterson (NJ) Police Department

"…a study in story telling, patience, character and plot development, and dedication to the craft of writing. But most importantly, it's a damn fine murder mystery."

Prof. Jean LeBlanc, author of *A Field Guide to the Spirits*

LAID SO LOW

"Mr. Bachman, a high school teacher loved by his students not because of what he teaches, but because he presents them with a model of compassion, decency, and humanity, an Atticus Finch of the Jersey shore… Sex trafficking is at the center of this page turner, as Mr. Bachman races to save a child from predators. Highly recommended.

J. P. Sattin

"We get a lot more focus on Mr. Bachman, with compelling prose and plotting and especially great use of dialog. Now I feel like I know this guy, and I care about him. I also enjoyed a fast paced, hard-to-put-down read of a heart-wrenching plot".

Phil Bookman, author of the *Mike Gold Mystery Series*

"Loved LAID SO LOW even more than [HEARTLESS CRUELTY]. I loved the complexity of the plot, the boldness of it, and the wonderful characters. Bravo!"

Prof. Priscilla Orr, author of *Losing the Horizon*

Pre-release Review of TAKEOVER
by industry veteran Bruce Apar

"Goffman, a veteran of the video wars, deftly blends strong story-telling skills with a breezy, friendly prose style that is just plain fun to read. Anyone who has worked at a company selling widgets, or in any kind of office for that matter, will recognize and appreciate the colorful cast of characters who bring Stellar Video and Circular Media to vivid life. Video, movie and record company workers along with pop music legends and movie stars may recognize among this crazy cast of characters friends and coworkers from years past.

"The reader is treated to a picturesque tale teeming with relatable, amusing moments that propel you into the gossip-driven world of the often-dysfunctional, always warring workplace.

"TAKEOVER will take over your undivided attention, so my advice is to finish it in one sitting, popcorn at the ready, as if you were sinking your teeth into a dishy DVD."

Bruce Apar, Award-Winning Business Journalist

Table of Contents

takeover

Prologue

1996

FADE IN:

EXT. - OCEAN - NIGHT

Pounding waves fill the screen. We could be
in the middle of the Atlantic, though we
can't tell anything because there are no
landmarks, just violently heaving water, an
amorphous image of ultimate power and utter
chaos. In the dark, it's hard to tell when
the waves are up and when they're down, and
the overall sensation is somewhat
disorienting. Finally, when we think we
can't take it anymore, the camera begins to
slowly pull back, and tilt. To our surprise,
we see we are only a hundred yards, at most,
from shore.

Now, the clouds shift and the darkness is
breached by moonlight. The narrow beam of
light from the dead orb reflects a dazzling

necklace on the dancing wavetops, and
illuminates a swath of beach. Other lights
stationed at regular intervals are clearly
man made.

Our eyes adjust. We're looking at the
beachfront of a mid-level resort hotel
somewhere in the Caribbean. Except for the
lighted walkways and entrances, and a
floodlight bathing a large pool and
surrounding deck, the hotel appears to
sleep. All the lights in all the rooms are
out.

Actually, that's not entirely true. One
room, on the northeast corner, on the 9th
floor, which is the top floor, has a light
of some sort on. The room is not fully lit,
but a flashlight, or perhaps a desk lamp,
maybe set down on the floor. As we float
closer to this window, there seems to be
some shadowy activity, some movement going
on in this room, while the rest of the hotel
guests sleep.

INT. - HOTEL CORRIDOR - NIGHT

FURTIVE MAN (P.O.V.)

moves as quietly as he can along the hotel
hallway. He passes Room 919, Room 921, 923.
We can see that he is heading for the
extreme end of the hallway, to the last
room, which isn't on the left or the right,
but directly facing us. This person, whose
face we can't see, moves with stealth. When
he hears a sound from behind Room 923 he
freezes and hugs the wall. After a moment he
completes his journey.

TAKEOVER

The room at the end is adorned with a professionally designed poster.

INSERT - POSTER

STELLAR VIDEO
NATIONAL SALES MEETING
1996
THE YEAR OF LIVING DANGEROUSLY

Below this, in slightly smaller letters:

STELLAR WELCOMES
CIRCULAR RECORDS

TOGETHER WE WELCOME
THE FUTURE OF
HOME ENTERTAINMENT

INSERT - POSTER

On the wall to the left of the door is another poster from a movie. There's an image of a soldier's combat helmet. Underneath the helmet is a simple legend:

WAR ROOM.

The FURTIVE MAN knocks quietly on the door, two short knocks, a pause, two more, another pause, then one. He waits. Then he pounds the door loudly with his fist.

> FURTIVE MAN
> (In a loud whisper)
> Come on you shmucks! Cut the James Bond crap and let me in, or I'm going back to sleep!

We see movement behind the peephole, we hear muttering from inside, and the sound of a chain being released and a lock being undone. The door opens into the mostly dark room, and the MAN enters.

CUT TO:

INT. - HOTEL SUITE - NIGHT

A bedside lamp has indeed been placed on the floor. This is the only light source in this suite, aside from the moonlight coming in the window. Straight ahead is a large, beautifully appointed bedroom with a king sized bed that has not been unmade so far tonight. Through a door to our left is an even larger conference room. In the middle of the room is a huge oak conference table, on which there are computers, laptops, printers, copiers, cameras, paper, cables, phones, cell phones, dozens of Red Stripe Beer bottles, ashtrays, half-eaten room service droppings, and assorted detritus. The wall alongside the conference table is decorated with printed sheets of paper, photographs, charts, schedules, lists of all sorts, hundreds of things taped to the flocked wallpaper, no doubt in violation of the hotel decorator's sensibilities. Obviously, some furious work has taken place recently inside this "War Room."

Now we can see that there are seven people in the room. They are grouped on the side of the room opposite from the conference table, on couches, chairs, the floor. We can't see any of their faces clearly, except their mouths and the bottoms of their noses, as they are lit from below. They speak softly,

in a tone that is urgent and conspiratorial.
Although clearly some of them view the cloak
and dagger aspects of the gathering with wry
amusement, others are deadly serious. In
this dim light an observer could not be
certain, but it might appear that five or
perhaps six of them are men; one, possibly
two are women.

> FIRST MAN
> OK, this is definitely
> happening now. I don't think
> anybody still thinks it won't
> happen?
>> (He pauses, but no one
>> disagrees.)
>
> So what are we going to do?

> SECOND MAN
> I've seen this before. I
> think I'm the only one here
> who has gone through this
> before, right?

> FIRST WOMAN
> Okay. And...?

> SECOND MAN
> Well, nothing will happen
> until there's ink on paper.
> That won't be for a few more
> months, at least.

> SECOND WOMAN
> Meanwhile, they're figuring
> out what to do with us.

FIRST WOMAN
They're used to servicing the whole country out of one location. We have eleven shipping points. Will they start doing it our way? Will all our warehouses start carrying CDs?

THIRD MAN
The first problem will be computer compatibility. I've talked to their IT people. They seem pretty cool, but I'm pretty sure our system is better than theirs.

SECOND MAN
Listen to me, all of you. It doesn't matter if our system is better than theirs. We'll have to learn theirs. It doesn't matter if our marketing and our magazines and our salespeople are better than theirs - I'm not saying they are or aren't, but just for argument's sake - our marketing, our publications, and our sales policies will start looking like theirs. And all of us will be reporting to one of them.

FOURTH MAN
But what about areas in which we're stronger? Surely they aren't going to interfere in

FOURTH MAN (continues)
the video side, in our
relationships with our
customers.

SECOND MAN
Please, you have got to
understand this. Circular is
buying Stellar. Not the other
way around. Not a "merger" as
Ernie keeps calling it. This
is a buyout.
And a buyout is like a war
between barbarian tribes.
First, the conquerors kill a
few of the conquered, to
demonstrate exactly who is in
charge. Next they kill off
one group after another, as
they determine what they do
and see that they can take it
over themselves. Ultimately,
they keep the best-looking
women, a few of the children,
and a handful of men for
slaves. And that's it.
Conquered. *Far-tik.*

FIRST WOMAN
I take it you are speaking
metaphorically there.

SECOND MAN
Yeah, but it's true.

FIRST MAN
That's one awfully gloomy
picture you're painting.
Maybe it doesn't always—

FIRST MAN is interrupted by the ringing of a telephone (o.s.). Everyone turns to look at THIRD MAN.

> SECOND WOMAN
> What the- ? Who the hell is calling you at three in the morning?

There is general shushing all around, and when it's completely quiet, THIRD MAN answers the phone, pretending to sound as if he has just been awakened.

> THIRD MAN
> Hello - who is it?
> (pause)
>
> What?
> (pause)
>
> Dude, what the fuck are you waking me up for?
> (pause)
>
> Really?
> (pause)
>
> Really?
> (pause)
>
> Well that must have been nice.
> (longer pause)
>
> You got that shit locally? Man, you're nuts. I'm glad you're not calling me to come

>   THIRD MAN (continues)
> bail you out from a Montego
> Bay jail.
>   (pause)
>
> No man. Thanks, maybe on
> Saturday night, when I can
> relax. Right now I got too
> much on my mind, and I have
> got to get back to sleep.
>   (pause)
>
> No, it's ok, I had to pee
> anyhow. Thanks for the offer.
> See you at breakfast in a
> couple of hours.

(THIRD MAN hangs up the phone.)

>   In case anybody's curious,
> Stevenson has some killer
> weed.
>   (Some laughter and tsk-
>   tsking from the group.)
>
> And Jane Sullivan took off
> her top at a party in T.C.'s
> room.
>   (More laughter, sounds of
>   amazement.)

>   SECOND WOMAN
> Lovely.

>   FIRST MAN
> That party sounds like it was
> more fun than this one.
> Anybody want a beer?

                    FOURTH MAN
Why isn't Stevenson here,
anyway?

                    FIRST WOMAN
He's not here because he
wasn't invited.

                    SECOND MAN
And he wasn't invited because
none of us trusts his smarmy,
kiss-ass, fake-tanned self.
        (General, almost cheerful
        agreement sounds from the
        group.)

Which brings us back to why
we're here. I think I can
wrap this up in a bow for
everyone so we can get a
little sleep.
First issue is Trust. We're
all here because we trust one
another. If anybody doesn't
feel that way about everybody
else in the room, speak up
right now.
        [A long, deadly silence]

Fine. Good. We trust one
another.

                    FIRST WOMAN
        (Exhaling)
Well, at least that wasn't
awkward.

                    SECOND MAN
Second issue is The Future.
For the first time in a long

SECOND MAN (continues)
time for most of us, the
future is very cloudy.
Chances are things are gonna
get bad. And after that
they're gonna get worse. We
all have wives or husbands
and kids or boyfriends or
girlfriends or cats or dogs
or birds or whatever. We have
our lives, our own interests
to consider. One thing is for
sure: Fallow and Fishbein
don't give a shit about
anybody they haven't had on
their team. Because that's
who They trust.

SECOND WOMAN
And don't count on B&E to be
looking out for anyone other
than B&E.

THIRD MAN
So what can we do?

SECOND MAN
Nothing. There's really not
much we can do, let's put it
that way, to change what's
gonna come down on us. But
one thing we can do is to
make sure we talk to each
other.

FIRST WOMAN
So what? We talk to each
other all the time anyhow.

FOURTH MAN

No, I get what you're saying. We've got to keep our eyes and ears open-

SECOND WOMAN

Keep each other informed.

FIRST MAN

Back each other up.

SECOND MAN

This is what I'm saying. We may not be able to stop them from picking us off one by one. But we need to be a step ahead of them in terms of knowing what's going on.

THIRD MAN

Does this really have to be so hostile? Maybe this will be a good thing in the end.

SECOND MAN

If this turns out to be the first takeover in corporate history to be benevolent and humanistic and kind, then talking to each other and keeping informed won't do any harm. But if, as is more likely, that's not the case, the more we watch each other's backs and keep each other informed, the better we'll come out of it. See what I'm saying?

TAKEOVER

FIRST WOMAN
Clearly, you're right. And
you know I don't often like
to agree with you.

FIRST MAN
...or anyone else.

The sound of general agreement in the room.
Then, speaking up for the first time...

FIFTH MAN
So, we're talking about a
pact. A solemn pact among the
seven of us.

FIRST MAN
Are we gonna sign in blood?
Because I get a little
queasy....

FIFTH MAN
I don't think we need to sign
anything, do we? We all know
who we are. Right?
(Silence)

But let's just be sure we
know what we're agreeing to.

SECOND WOMAN
We're agreeing to watch each
other's backs.

FIFTH MAN
Right. And what does that
consist of?

> SECOND WOMAN
Anything we hear that may affect any one of us, or anybody else we care about, we let each other know as soon as possible.

> FIFTH MAN
Good. What else?

> FIRST MAN
We agree that this meeting remains secret. Like it never happened. Nobody but us knows about it, and that's how it should stay.

> FIRST WOMAN and FOURTH MAN
What meeting?

> FIFTH MAN
Exactly. Good. Anything else?

> FIRST WOMAN
We do our best to support each other in front of them. Even when we disagree in private.

> SECOND WOMAN
Isn't that sort of like what I said?

> FIFTH MAN
No, it's not. And it's important, too. Anything else?

SECOND MAN
Yeah, and this may be the
most important of all. What
we have in our heads, They
will need. So the first thing
they're gonna start to do,
they're gonna try and
download us. Now we can't act
like we don't know anything,
they know we know stuff, they
know we're not morons. But be
careful what you give away,
and don't give away any of
our tricks, or anything they
won't think of to ask about.
And don't let them piggyback
on your relationships, if you
can help it. Don't give up
any of this shit, until the
day that we all get back
together and decide it's time
to trust Them.

FIFTH MAN
Good. Great. I think we've
got it. One: Share
information. Two: Keep our
alliance secret. Three: Boost
each other's reputation to
Them whenever we can. And
Four: Be as tightfisted as we
can with information because
information is power. Anybody
think we ought to write it
down?

THIRD MAN
We don't need to write it
down. Anybody think you're

RICHARD W. GOFFMAN

                    THIRD MAN (continues)
          gonna forget any of those
          four things?

Again there is the sound of general
agreement in the room.

                    THIRD MAN
          Boys and girls, I think we're
          done here.

                    FIFTH MAN
          Wait.

                    FIRST MAN and SECOND WOMAN
          What?

                    FIFTH MAN
          Anybody care to make this
          interesting?

                    FIRST WOMAN
          Are you nucking futs? This
          isn't "interesting" enough
          already?

                    FIFTH MAN
          Everybody got a business card
          on them?
              (They all do.)

          Let's pick a date in the
          future - say a year - no,
          three years from now. Write
          all seven of our names on the
          back, and write where you
          think each of us will be on
          that date.

THIRD MAN
You're right. This night is
something that we're all
gonna look back on as a
turning point, one way or the
other. In three years we all
get together and see who came
closest.
    (General positive hubbub.)

SECOND WOMAN
How about three years and
four months?

THIRD MAN
Why? What the hell is that?

SECOND WOMAN
I'm talking about December
31, 1999.

FIFTH MAN
End of the millennium.
Perfect. Where will each of
us be when the new millennium
begins?

FIRST MAN
It's kinda like one of those
death pools.

FIRST WOMAN
Christ, let's hope not.

FOURTH MAN
And the winner gets?

FIRST MAN
We all put in a hundred
bucks, and the person who has

     FIRST MAN (continues)
the closest guesses gets it
all.

     FIRST WOMAN
Whoa there, Kemosabe! I'm
only a poor corrupt official.

     FIFTH MAN
The money's only symbolic,
just to make it interesting.
How's $50?

     SECOND WOMAN
Winner gets $350?

     FIRST WOMAN
That's pretty interesting.

They all take money out of their wallets and
give it to FIFTH MAN, who puts it in a
manila envelope he picks up from the
conference table. Then they all take out
business cards and pens, and each person
seeks a spot in the room in which to sit and
write, and in which to contemplate the other
six.

     FIRST MAN
What about ourselves?

     FIFTH MAN
Absolutely. That's the most
interesting prediction of
all.

     SECOND WOMAN
Who's got the most insight
into themself, eh? Hmmm....

The FIFTH MAN drops his card in the envelope first, and then walks around the room accepting cards from the others as they finish.

CUT TO:

EXT. - HOTEL BEACHFRONT - NIGHT (PRE-DAWN)

The sky has already begun to lighten, as we look at the hotel from the same vantage point as we first saw it. Color is starting to seep back into everything. A couple of the other rooms with early risers have switched on their lights, and someone is jogging on the beach.

Now we really can't tell whether there are lights on or not, as the sun comes over the hotel, brightening everything. Our view gets brighter and whiter until it's all bleached out white. As white as Part One, Chapter One, Page One of a brand new expensively printed and bound novel.

PART I
THE TAKEOVER

Chapter One
Soft Landing

1997

ITHINK THE HYPNOTIST REALLY DID HELP YOU."
It took George Becker a moment to figure out what this meant, a second moment to determine who had said it, and then one more to realize where he was sitting while hearing it. He was sitting in coach, on Continental flight 1410, flying west across the Atlantic toward John F. Kennedy International Airport, away from Charles deGaulle Airport, and the author of this not-so-enigmatic statement was his seatmate, Alice May Buford-Becker, his wife. She was the only person he knew who would begin speaking to him, in a conversational tone, while he was sound asleep, fully expecting him to respond as though he were awake. What Alice May was talking about was the fact that her husband had been able to sleep so peacefully on the flight.

In fact, it was remarkable that George was able to even sit still on this flight, that he had been able to wholly enjoy himself on their vacation in France, and that he had such a calm expression on his face. George, now fully awake, thought about it carefully and agreed.

"I didn't think she'd done me any good at all. At first. But I think maybe you're right." Apparently, Dr. Mandy Potranowitz, the hypnotist he'd gone to see in desperation to help him with his fear of flying, had helped after all. The very fact that he had to think about it pretty much proved it. In the last two years he'd flown twenty-five or thirty times, and in each case he had arrived a physical and emotional wreck, exhausted from desperately gripping the seat arms and whipping his head around frantically trying to find someone's face who didn't seem at all concerned that they were all about to die and who looked like someone whose intelligence George might be able to trust. If he couldn't find a fellow passenger, bored, doing a crossword puzzle or playing solitaire or laughing at the movie, he'd try to spot a baby. A sweet innocent baby. Because how could God let the plane go down with such a beautiful, angelic innocent on board? If this was his only solace, he used it, even though he knew damn well that God killed babies every day. By the fistful.

1995

HE HADN'T ALWAYS BEEN LIKE THIS. IT ALL BEGAN with a flight two years earlier, all ready to come in ahead of schedule, getting George home from a business trip to Las Vegas. In those days, traveling as much as he did, flying was almost a bore. Almost. He had to admit that he still got a little of the thrill from it – back then – like the excitement he'd felt when he was younger and flew only rarely. He liked looking out the window (he'd long since switched his preference to the aisle seat, where he could at least expand his elbow and crossed legs an inch extra) and trying to identify formations on the ground. He liked pretending he was one of the Mercury astronauts, zipping along in Friendship 7, looking back at the earth from a vantage no one had ever had before.

On the Vegas-to-Newark flight George had been seated among a family – wife, husband, two daughters – who were also returning home to New Jersey. This family was returning not from a vacation, but a funeral, and they were all still subdued by their sadness. For the parents, whose names he still remembered, Stanley and Aurora Chesterton, the trip to Las Vegas had been their first time ever inside an airplane, and this return flight, three days later, was their second. Aurora was seated next to George, and Stanley and his daughters were directly behind them. The girls took care of Stan, and George talked Aurora through the takeoff and the occasional minor turbulence.

It had been an almost entirely uneventful flight. Even the weather, which had been nasty in Newark just a few hours before they'd taken off from Las Vegas, had been cooperative, clearing nicely, leaving only a few puddles and a beautiful windswept clear sky. Their descent followed the normal path, right over the New Jersey Turnpike, northbound. Though it was after eleven at night east coast time, George could make out Ikea's giant roof, and the huge BRUUUUCE! banner hung from the Continental Airlines Arena in the Meadowlands, welcoming Jersey's favorite son for a two-week stint of shows. He was about to warn Aurora that the landing gear would make a sound when the captain engaged them, but it happened before he could get the words out, and the seat belt, fastened low and tight across her lap, was the only thing that kept Aurora from leaping from her middle seat. She grabbed his left hand tightly, and she didn't let go when George explained the source of the noise.

Now they were almost down. They were lower than some of the buildings across the Hudson, they could make out individuals in the cars on the Turnpike if they had their interior lights on. The big jet, a United 777, not that it mattered, made a gentle, almost pleasant left-right movement, dipping first one wing slightly, then the other. At the first sign of this Aurora gripped George's hand tighter. He thought his pinky was going to be dislocated, which distracted him for a second from the fact that the left-right rocking motion repeated itself, this time with a slightly deeper dip on each side. They were low enough now, and slowed enough, that they were being "passed" by some of the cars below them.

The oscillation of the plane continued, and George was not the only frequent flyer on board who noticed that each rock and roll was a bit more than the one before. He couldn't be sure how far they were from the runway, but it seemed to him that it couldn't be very far at all. A few hundred feet? Well shit, what's the length of this plane's wing? George's left hand was numb in Aurora's now crushing grip. They were still descending, and they were now rocking back and forth so extremely that stuff was flying around the cabin. Simultaneously, without consulting with one another, Stan and his wife began to sing a hymn, loudly, clearly expecting this to be their last moments, and hoping to die with Jesus' name on their lips. That was all it took for the resolve of the rest of the passengers to disappear completely, and shrieks and shouted prayers rang out all over the plane. George noticed with incredulity that he was now also holding hands with a Pakistani businessman seated across the aisle, though he didn't know how long they'd been grasping each other.

Now the rocking was ridiculous. The left wing went down so low that George's extended right arm, attached to his Pakistani neighbor, seemed to be pointing straight upward. Looking to his left, past Aurora whose fervent appeals to God were now silent, he could see the tip of the wing, and he could see the ground, and the latter could not be much further away than the former. Certainly, if this left-right motion continued to increase with each rock, the left wing would touch the ground the next time it went down. What would happen then? George's mind shut out the now constant cacophony of screaming, which drowned out the sound of the jet's engines as he envisioned Alice May, blue bathrobe belted tight, eyes sunken in shock and despair, sitting at their dining room table, nodding numbly as a pair of faceless men described to her how the wingtip of United Flight 1202 hit the runway before the landing gear; how the plane had at that point continued in its direction, but cartwheeling, wing, nose, wing, tail, wing, nose—Alice May, always the realist, would want to know precisely what had taken place; how it had then gone to pieces, hurling pieces of plane and clumps of passengers hundreds of yards in every direction, like wooden horses spun off by the centrifugal force of a carousel gone amok. Some bodies were found in the Meadowlands parking lot, some were across the Turnpike, in a rest area. Yes, she'd be ready to come identify George's remains, just as soon as she could wake someone up to come stay with the kids.

The screaming in the cabin was similar to what you would hear on a roller coaster, rising and falling with the rocking of the plane, only without the undercurrent of ironic laughter after each burst of screaming. The right wing went down. Incredibly, it didn't hit the ground. They rocked back up and to the left. George noticed for the first time that a flight attendant was lying face down in the aisle, beneath his and the Pakistani's outstretched arms, her skirt somehow up over her torso. As the left wing began to make what surely had to be its final dip, George felt, and then heard, the big jet's engines straining. The whole plane shuddered violently. It seemed to bend, to arch its back. The leftward dip was not as great as he expected it to be, but the plane was still getting closer to the ground, and still rocking. And then it wasn't getting closer to the ground, it was curving back upward. Or trying to. George looked past Aurora out the window to his left, and saw a member of the ground crew, the ping-pong paddle guys, watching. He thought he could see the man's expression of horror at what he was witnessing. He waved his paddles wildly. George felt like he made eye contact with the guy, but that must have been impossible. But he knew he saw one freaked out crew member who was darting around erratically, wanting to run for his life but unsure of which direction to run.

They could all now feel the plane's engines and feel the struggle to abort the landing and climb back upward into the relative safety of the sky. *Go! Up! Up! Up where there was nothing solid to smash into at 150 miles per hour!* George imagined the beads of sweat on the face of the pilot as he pulled back on the controls, the strength of his arm and back muscles the only thing that could save them all. The plane shuddered, as if it would come apart from the stress of all these violent changes of direction, all these conflicting vectors. They reached the bottom of their parabola and started upward, the jet still shuddering in protest. And then they weren't rocking at all anymore, and they weren't shuddering anymore, and they were heading back up into the sky at a 45 degree angle.

Most of the screaming had stopped, George wasn't sure when, and all that could be heard was a few people crying quietly. They continued upward, quietly, for at least another minute before everyone disengaged their hands from each other. Joanne, the flight attendant, got bravely to her feet, affecting a nonchalance that was belied by her pallor, offset by a trickle of blood from her nose. George handed her a napkin and pointed to her nose; Tariq, the guy across the aisle, discreetly drew the hem of her skirt down without her realizing it had gone up.

The shuddering had stopped, and the jet continued to ascend. The pilot was back in control. It was only then, after what seemed like ten minutes but was probably only a matter of ten or twenty seconds, that the captain's voice came over the speakers in the cabin, in its inevitable Texas drawl.

"You may have noticed a rough bit back there," he began. Finally amazed laughter and curses burst from the passengers at the incredible understatement. The captain went on to explain that there was some rough air left over from the earlier storm, and that because it was right at ground level it had escaped detection by radar. They would be making a circle and coming back in and landing properly. It was a big circle. George could tell that they were at a higher altitude than planes waiting to land normally ascend to. He had circled Newark many times before waiting to land, but never had that circle extended far out over Long Island to the east, and as far west as Paterson. At last, as they began to approach Newark Airport again, the co-pilot came on and reassured everyone that there was now no turbulence at all, on the ground or anywhere, and that they would be on the tarmac in a few seconds. That sucked all the whispering out of the cabin. George realized for the first time that he and Aurora were still holding hands, they had never let go, and he was glad. He didn't look over at Tariq. He pictured Alice May, and Sally and Will, their daughter and son. And then they were on the ground.

Home. George walked into the bedroom where Alice May snored lightly. It was almost three am. He had absolutely no recollection of the cab ride, and he was glad to see that, though he couldn't remember doing it, he had retrieved his suitcase. In all previous instances when he came home late from a trip he always tried to slip in quietly, his goal being to undress and snuggle up to his wife under the covers before she realized that he was home. This time though, he placed his suitcase on the floor, walked to his side of the bed, and switched on the light. "Alice May. Please wake up, because I never thought I was going to ever see you again."

1997

THAT WAS THEN. NOW, AIR FRANCE 220 LANDED LIKE a feather, five minutes ahead of schedule, and George could not even have told you if there were any children on the flight. The driver met them promptly, and helped with all the bags. Within an hour they were in Teaneck. Sally was with a dozen other international campers in Kenya, Will was on a cross-country road trip doing God knows what, and Pavlov, their mutt, was at Grandma and Grampa's. Although it was only

6:30 p.m., to them it was the wee hours of the next morning. "*Je suis fatiguè*," said Alice May, repeating the one sentence in French that George had learned thoroughly. After munching on something, they slept.

Chapter Two
Bastille Day Already?

1997

ON SATURDAY, GEORGE GOT IN THE CAR TO GO TO THE post office to pick up the mail. There was a ton of it, a whole bin full. They hadn't taken a two-week vacation in more than ten years. The most remarkable thing about the trip, George realized as he continued through town, picking up a few groceries, waving to some neighbors he saw walking their dogs, was that he'd been able to relax almost completely. This was always a challenge for him, relaxing while on vacation instead of worrying about what was going on back at work. It should have been particularly challenging now, as the big buyout had just been completed. Stellar Video Dist., L.P., the company he'd worked for for the past eighteen years, had just been acquired by Circular Records, a music distributor from northern California. Everyone he worked with at Stellar was freaking out. They were sure they were going to be replaced, demoted, laid off, betrayed, lied to, and screwed, not necessarily in that order; they were suspicious of every move, every memo, every word, that emanated from Circular headquarters in Davis, CA.

Everyone was freaking out except George. George was
Stellar's VP of Marketing. His bosses, the owners – *former*
owners – of Stellar, Ernest Lehrer and Herbert Jacobs, had
relied on him heavily. No one knew if Bert and Ernie, as they
were universally known throughout the company and
throughout the video industry, would stay on as employees in
the company they had built, the first of its kind in the US. It was
hard to picture them having to answer to someone, especially
someone who lived and worked in California and had almost no
relationships, good or bad, among the movie studio executives
or the video store chain owners and buyers. But George wasn't
freaking out.

George wasn't freaking out because he'd long felt he'd hit
the ceiling at work. Not a glass ceiling, but a steel ceiling, one
that could not be broken through. Bert and Ernie would never
make him a partner, and they already paid him pretty well and
were not likely to give him more than incremental raises in the
future. But now that Stellar was becoming a division of Circular,
George wasn't at the ceiling any more. There was a floor above
his head, populated by Circular execs. None of them knew the
video business as he and his friends at Stellar did. They did
know the music business, inside and out. Maybe George would
get to learn that business, while helping them to understand his.
Maybe work would become interesting again.

To George, becoming part of Circular was exciting. They
had concerts in the lobby of their office. Dylan had played two
songs there the last time he had a new studio album out. Brian
Fallow, the Circular CEO, and Arthur Fishbein, its owner and
founder, were important guests at the Grammys each year. Bert
and Ernie never went to the Oscars. Circular was happening.

Circular was a corporation, and that sounded exciting to
George. He had learned the abbreviation HR since visiting
Circular HQ. It was what they called the human resources
department. Human resources recruited employees, set up all
sorts of programs for employees, helped out in the community,
planned parties, took care of benefits. There were 61 people in

Circular's HR department, and a senior VP of HR. They had their own wing. At Stellar, one individual, Judy Frink, was in charge of payroll, benefits, setting up the annual Christmas party, making Bert and Ernie's coffee three times a day, making their plane reservations, balancing Bert's personal checking account, typing for the two of them, sorting their mail, and sitting at the front desk and answering the switchboard when Amelia, the regular receptionist, had lunch or needed to pee.

The fact that he would be working for a company that had a 61-person HR department instead of an HR "department" of about half a person seemed to George to be a good harbinger. He looked forward to finding out what other differences there would be as he moved into a professional company from a "mom-and-pop." Many in the video business compared Stellar and its owners to a Lower East Side men's clothing store. Only this clothing store happened to have done three-quarters of a million bucks in pants and sport coats last year.

George had great affection for Bert and Ernie, more Bert than Ernie if truth be told. Both had made his life hell for the first year he'd worked for them. He remembered his first day as a full time employee. As he was settling into his new office – the first time in his life that he had ever *had* an office – organizing supplies, outlining plans and priorities – Ernie had poked his head in to welcome him to the team. "Listen," Ernie had said. "Take your time. Get the lay of the land. Don't try to make too many big changes all at once. We hired you to improve how we do stuff, but first you gotta get a feel for what works and what doesn't. Gradually you'll put your mark on things."

Less than five minutes after Ernie left the room, Bert arrived at work. He stopped in to see George on his first day on the job. "Look kid, I'm glad you're here. We're leaving a ton of money on the table, I'm sure of it. Don't waste any time. We brought you here to make changes, and you should start immediately. Turn this place upside down if you have to. Just tell me what you need and you'll get it."

The diametrically opposite marching orders from the

owners made George feel as though whatever he did would please one boss and piss off the other. But eventually he got them, and they got him. After that, they left him alone. In each position he'd had at Stellar he made them money, and that was all you needed to do to be given the measure of freedom that George enjoyed. If he wanted to spend $20,000 for a couple of new computers, he'd make an Excel spreadsheet showing that they'd pay for themselves in six months and continue paying after that, leave it on their desks, and go out and order them the next day. If he wanted to hire a salesperson or an artist or a techie, he'd let them know about it after he'd interviewed and found the right one. He'd introduce the prospective employee (after warning him, or especially her, about B&E's manner and how not to take it seriously) to one or the other of them. They'd chat with the person for a few minutes and send them on their way. In the last ten years they had never disagreed with him on a new hire.

So it was unusual that George, who normally had a hard time relaxing on vacation, who often called in just to make sure things were going okay, spent very little time thinking about business during the two weeks they'd spent in France, the first in Paris, at a charming hotel in the 6th *arrondissement*, the second in an apartment Alice May had procured in Aix en Provence, a modern one bedroom flat inside a building that went up in the 15th century. Particularly unusual since there was so much turbulence, so much change going on at work. Maybe it was a by-product of the hypnotist's work. Maybe it was the distraction of the City of Light and the rolling hills of lavender and grapes in wine country. Maybe it was Alice May, who said to him in the cab on the way to the airport two weeks before, "Listen. You *are* going to relax this time. And just remember this: the last time you took off two weeks in a row, and you were so worried about it, and you couldn't call in because there was no phone at the cabin, what happened?" The question was apparently rhetorical, because she plunged on without waiting for his response. "When you got back, they gave you more responsibility and a big fat raise. Remember?"

Whatever it was, it was good. Though so many were wracked with insecurity, George was strangely calm. For one thing, he had met enough of the folks at Circular that he was neither intimidated nor unimpressed. They seemed generous in welcoming the Stellar people, friendly in a sort of dry, chilly way, and willing to listen. Best of all, they didn't know jack shit about the video business. It was clear that he and many of his best friends were going to be indispensable in this new music-plus-video distribution company.

George nosed the Accord into the driveway and around back of the house. He tossed the couple of grocery items into the big box of mail, and, noticing his wife looking at him from the kitchen window, exaggerated the weight of the very substantial load. "God damn, we're popular!" is what he said when he'd schlepped it all inside.

"Don't get too excited," Alice May replied. "It's probably mostly junk."

"You're probably right, but there sure is a lot of it. I'll sort through it in a bit. I just want to call my folks and tell them when we're coming to pick up Pavlov."

Alice May called after him as he walked up the stairs with the mail, heading for their study. "You may want to check your messages. There are a lot."

"What's 'a lot'?"

"Well, there were many more than I expected. Seventeen I think, which is strange since everybody knew we'd be away. One was from my department secretary, one was from Rebecca at MacMillan, and the other fifteen sounded like they were from your work. I could tell they weren't for me, because my messages don't normally start with the word 'Dude!' I didn't listen to those, I just saved them for you."

The hair stood up on the back of George's neck. What the hell could all this be about? He'd been resolute in his determination to relax and rejuvenate while on vacation in spite of everything… Maybe that had been a bad idea after all? Maybe he should have heeded his normal inclination to worry and call the office every couple of days? He started considering all the disasters that could have taken place while he was away. Even so, everybody knew he wouldn't be home to receive these calls, so what the...

He remembered something that he'd put out of his mind. A few days before he left on vacation, he had gotten an e-mail from Davis, from Angela Crofut, the Sr. VP of HR.

> FROM: AAC
> TO: GWB
> RE: Emergency contact info
> Hi George! :) How could we get in touch with you, just in case there was an emergency? Bri would like to have that if you could, phone and fax.
> Thanks, and have a great trip!!! I can't wait to really start working with all you guys. Great things are happening!!! :)
>
> Angela A. Crofut
> Senior Vice President, Human Resources
> Circular Records, Inc.
> 6000 Pole Line Road
> Davis, CA 95616

What the fuck? George and Angela never spoke before he left, but the e-mail messages ping-ponged across the country.

> FROM: GWB
> TO: AAC
> RE: RE: Emergency contact info
> Hi Angela. Thanks, we will have a great time, I think. Alice May took an intensive French class, and I am definitely going to relax.
> Speaking of relaxing, I've been going full tilt for almost a year and a half, and I promised my wife a vacation where I don't call in and I don't think about the office.

Please let me know if this is really important. Thanks.
George

FROM: AAC
TO: GWB
RE: RE: RE: Emergency contact info
Oh no, George, you needn't call in, and you definitely
deserve your downtime. ;)
I'm sure he won't call, it's just that, there's so much
going on, Brian just would appreciate if you would just
go ahead and shoot us the numbers of your hotels. Just
in case. Thanks. With everything going on, and you
being so important in this transition, I think he'd just
feel better knowing he could reach out to you if he
wanted to. I'm sure he won't.

Angela A. Crofut
Senior Vice President, Human Resources
Circular Records, Inc.
6000 Pole Line Road
Davis, CA 95616

The folks at Stellar hadn't had email for long, but he knew
the signature at the bottom was an automatic function, not put
there specifically by Angela to remind him she outranked him.
Hell, he should feel flattered that Fallow wanted to be able to
reach him, any time, anywhere. Another reassurance that he was
a key player. A keeper. Still, he did not want, at this point, to
appear overawed by the Californians.

FROM: GWB
TO: AAC
RE: RE: RE: RE: Emergency contact info

OK, no problem, thanks for explaining. I'll check with
Alice May tonight – she's in charge of all of that stuff –

and then I'll shoot you the info. But tell Brian not to call unless my office is on fire! (That's a joke.)

He didn't need to ask Alice May. He had a copy of all the hotel information in his briefcase. It just bothered him. George "forgot" to send the requested information until his last day at the office, but then he figured he ought to stop being paranoid. Pulling out the copy of their itinerary from his briefcase, he copied the phone number of the *Hôtel St. Germain*, and the phone number of the apartment, and the dates they would be at each place. And then, just before hitting Send, he had slid the cursor up to the hotel phone number, and changed its last digit by one. *Bon voyage!*

Surely that couldn't be what so many phone calls were about. When they'd come back from dinner the second night of their stay, George asked the concierge if there was a fax for him. There wasn't. He'd put it out of his mind. Now he dumped the box of mail onto the couch in the study, tossed the empty bin into the hall, and sat down at his desk. He took a new white lined pad from the bottom drawer and a pen from the jar, drew a deep, yogic breath, and hit the "play messages" button on the answering machine while staring at the frantically blinking little green light.

The first one was from Hakizimana Wasef – Hock to his friends – the head buyer: "Dude. Ernie's out. Bert left yesterday. Their initials on their parking spaces have already been painted over. Call me when you get back. Hope you had a nice trip – you picked one hell of a time to be away. Maybe a smart time. Call me."

George breathed half a sigh of relief. Clearly this was bullshit. He and Hock and quite a few of the other people at Stellar had a colorful and creative history of practical jokes they pulled on one another. One time they sent Lane Coutell on a totally bogus trip to Cleveland to visit a non-existent customer. Every time a practical joke was pulled on someone a series of revenge gags would ensue until things got ridiculous. Not only that, he now remembered, but people who went away on vacation were prime targets. Once he had returned from a business trip, not even a vacation, to find that his desk had been turned around. He didn't realize this until he sat down and slammed his legs into the back of it. They'd broken into his office (not in itself an impressive feat), rotated the desk 180 degrees, and then turned everything he kept on top of the desk back, so that all looked normal. As the day wore on, he found that all his calls had been forwarded to the phone in the supply room, and the calls that did come in to his extension were invariably for Annabelle, the colorful Filipino transvestite who worked in the warehouse. And his computer's screen saver, which he discovered after he had logged on and then stepped away to straighten out the phone extensions, read "Thanks for last night, loverman. Kisses, Annabelle." George knew that the best revenge on his practical jokers was to keep a straight face, fix everything back himself, and then pretend nothing had happened, that their plans had not worked. But he had to hand it to the guys, that one was funny.

So that's what this must be, this call from Hock. And now he felt pretty sure that the remaining fourteen messages would all be from different people supporting the gag. Still, he wrote down on the pad, "Call Hock," before deleting and going to the next message.

It was Hock again. "I almost forgot the best part. Bert's out. Ernie's out. Lane's *in*. Call me!"

Lane was "in." That was a good touch, because Lane Coutell, the sales VP who ran the Stockbridge, Massachusetts branch, was Bert and Ernie's longest-time employee, one of the few so-called "Stellar Lifers" who'd been there prior to George. Lane had an ego the size of a small planet. He had long expressed the belief that he would be tapped to run the company as soon as either Ernie or Bert decided to retire. Lane was a likeable enough guy if you didn't work under him, though not everyone who knew him agreed with his own self-assessment.

Bert and Ernie out, Lane in. Indeed. Bert and Ernie not running Stellar was impossible to picture. At the same time, it was what many, especially outside observers, predicted with the new acquisition (which Ernie continued to refer to as "the merger"). Really it was too believable to be believable. It was too on the nose. Hock and the boys would have to do better than this.

He pushed the answering machine button again. The next message was from Esperanza Isip, George's right hand person. Without his confidence in her, he'd never be able to take a couple of days off, let alone two whole weeks in a row. Esperanza wasn't always the formidable presence she'd evolved into since she had arrived at Stellar. When he first hired her, as a typesetter, she was timid, limited by a self-image that said, "This is the most I can be, and I'm lucky at that." She was incapable of dealing with disruptions to the normal flow of things. Luckily, George recognized qualities in her that she never suspected were there. Over time she learned that there was no "normal" flow of things, that if you were good at your job – and she was – that people listened to you, and then expected you to do bigger and better things. Today she could run the whole department if need be.

"George, I hope you're having a great trip, and I'm sorry to call you at home. But I want you to know that there have been a few major changes here, starting the day after you left, and you may want to know about them before you come in on the 28th. Brian Fallow came here, unannounced, just showed up that Monday morning. He climbed his scrawny ass – sorry – up onto a desk in the sales area, and called everyone around, and made some announcements. So if you want to hear about it before you come in, you can call me, 201-555-7623."

That was an impressive move, getting Groucho – that was Esperanza's office nickname – to call in furtherance of the guys' prank. That lent real verisimilitude, because she was such a no-nonsense person. He wondered what they'd bribed her with. But he was having difficulty imagining her lying to him, especially on a phone message. Maybe… Maybe it wasn't a lie? No, he shook it off as something just too preposterous to imagine on top of jet lag. And he wondered if every one of these messages was going to be about this gag, each one adding a little more information. He had to admit, the guys had gone to a lot of trouble on this one. Maybe on Monday he'd say that his answering machine had gone on the fritz while he was away, no messages at all. He'd like to see their faces when he let that slip out.

On the other hand...

All the rest of the messages were indeed about the abrupt departure of Bert and Ernie. Without accepting their veracity, he took notes while listening to all of them. Two of them separately quoted Fallow, standing on Tony Infante's desk in sales, intoning, "There will not be any more changes. All your jobs are safe." Some of the calls were from people outside the company who had heard about the events of Monday, July 14th and wanted to get his take on it. Andrea Battaglia from MGM and Artie Page from Disney both said that they thought that he, George, not Lane, was the "heir apparent." *Couple of suck-up troublemakers.* One was from Richie Orgone from *Video Retailer Magazine*, the weekly trade paper, asking for his comment. Richie rarely called him at home.

What elaborate bullshit.

George hit "delete all messages", and tore off the page from the pad. He started to put it aside, but then he looked at it again. July 14th. Their second day in Paris. *Bastille Day.*

He crumpled the sheet of paper, walked downstairs, and poured himself a large Scotch. After one sip he told himself that he wouldn't return any of the calls. Bullshit or not, he still had a day and a half before he jumped back into the maelstrom, and he was determined to finish his vacation as he had spent it: relaxing, not thinking about work.

Chapter Three
Meet the B Team

1997

AT A QUARTER TO SIX, TERRY LUNCEFORD DROPPED OFF Sammy, her sleepy-faced five-year-old son, at her mother's house. Mama's house was hell and gone at the other end of Bayonne, the opposite direction she needed to go in the morning. But ever since Mama had gotten out of the hospital with instructions not to drive "for a while," what else was she going to do? Besides, Sammy's school was as close to Mama's house than it was to their own, and there was a neighbor, a white lady who walked her daughter to kindergarten at the Parson Street School, and she was glad to take Sammy along.

So that end was covered. Mama seemed fine today, and with Terry's brother James back in town and staying there, she felt less inclined than usual to worry about her. Of course, she'd find other things to worry about. How long would James stay? What would happen when he left again, as he inevitably would? What would she do about Mama if she became truly incapacitated? Didn't Sammy's cold seem to be hanging around way too long? Who was the freak who had called three times last night, never said a word, and hesitated a moment each time before hanging up? What would this buyout or whatever it was at Stellar mean for her future?

Of all the worries Terry could list as she drove past Port Liberté and all the new construction, through the most tragic parts of Jersey City and up to the gate at the Stellar parking lot, it was the last one that seemed easiest to predict: she was going to get screwed, most likely sooner rather than later. She didn't give a shit what that skinny Brian Fallow in his stupid ass Bermuda shorts – *imagine? at work?* – had said when he'd stood on top of that desk. How stupid did he take all of them for? That's the part that was most insulting. She agreed with Tina, who at least had the balls to raise her hand when Fallow had "opened the floor for questions" and asked what was on everybody's mind.

"So, are you telling us that's a promise? How long is it good for?"

A look of amazement had rippled across many of the faces in the sales area, but Fallow hadn't even blinked, hadn't even varied his smile. "That's right, Tina. You have my word." He'd looked around then, dramatically, at everyone, seeming to make eye contact with every one of the one hundred twenty-odd people in the room. "There are no plans to close any facilities or lay any people off. This company – this brand new company, consisting of almost a thousand people who have already been working for Circular, and the 244 current Stellar employees – is gonna grow, not shrink. Our goal is to be a Billion Dollar Company by the year 2000! Do you think we're gonna do that with *fewer* people? Or *more* people?"

Everyone had looked at each other then, weighing what he'd said. *A billion dollar company?* Nobody was supposed to know the annual figures at Stellar, but Terry and lots of other people smart enough to figure it out knew that Bert and Ernie were coming off their best year yet, close to $300 million in gross sales. And it was common knowledge that, although Circular was the buyer and Stellar the bought, the video distributor had always done more business per year than the high profile music wholesaler. So as a combined entity they were going to double their business in less than three years? Ha! Terry glanced at three or four people in the room who she knew would have made the same mental calculations as quickly as she did and saw similar looks of incredulity on all of their faces. *Billion dollar company?* They must be planning on buying up a few more businesses pretty quick then because she couldn't see any way they were going to double sales. Of course, what the hell did she know? She was just a single mom who made maybe thirty-five grand a year working two jobs, neither one of which offered any security at all. Was she going to argue with a self-confident Captain of Industry?

Now she pulled up in front of Stellar HQ to do her only morning task – opening. Terry set the Subaru's hand brake and leaned over to pop the glove box. Pulling from it a jangly set of work keys on an old, green fabric strap with the words *One Flew over the Cuckoo's Nest* embroidered on it in white, she hopped out of the station wagon to do the hardest part of her duties at Stellar. She inserted the right key into the massive, five-pound padlock on the heavy-duty chain that kept the neighbors from opening the parking lot gate nearest Stellar's warehouse entrance. The old lock sprang open with a rusty "Clack." She disengaged the long, thick 120-grade chain from the sliding part of the gate, which, like the rest of the 10-foot-high steel fence surrounding Stellar was topped with rolls and rolls of looping, nasty-looking razor wire, and wrapped it a couple of times around the stationary post and relocked it there. Then, taking a deep breath of the already humid morning air, she leaned all her 110 pounds into her shoulder and her shoulder into the sliding gate. It always seemed that today was going to be the morning that it just was not going to budge, but in a few seconds it did, slowly and noisily. When she moved it all the way across the 12-foot opening, she looked down at her sweater and, though she saw nothing there, she brushed herself off before getting back into the car. Terry drove into the lot, parked in the spot nearest the door that didn't have an executive's initials painted on the blacktop, grabbed her shoulder bag, and hopped back out again, locking the car. Turning away from Stellar, she quickly walked the six blocks past the Liberty Street Project, crossed Eisenhower, and hurried to the Ultimate Diner to work the morning rush. She wouldn't get to her desk at Stellar until 11.

BOUNCING INTO THE ULTIMATE AT 6:45 WAS ALWAYS an uplifting moment, the moment when she really, finally felt awake. Terry greeted the other girls and the regulars at the counter. In the back she threw on her uniform, folded her jeans and sweater, put them inside the big shoulder bag and hoisted the bag up on top of the dessert refrigerator. Back out front in a flash, she poured two coffees, one for herself and one for Mr. Lai, whom she'd spotted heading their way as he did most mornings, not far behind her. She loved the look on the face of customers who sat down and saw what they hadn't yet asked for placed right in front of them; they always beamed at Terry with a mixture of gratitude and awe. As if knowing that Mr. Lai would want coffee with cream and Equal at ten to seven when he came in as he'd done a hundred times before was such an accomplishment. Jeez.

This Monday morning rush wasn't as bad as it could be, which was just as well so far as Terry was concerned. She knew she could make up for the smaller number of tips by increasing each one's value slightly, and not having to rush as much, she could easily do that. A big smile and a wink for Mr. Lai and some of the other old timers was worth about a buck apiece most of the time. At the Ultimate, a little harmless flirting paid a little, and every little bit helped.

About quarter past seven Terry put the hand-lettered cardboard RESERVED sign on table 14, the big round one in the alcove that bulged out of the corner of the restaurant. She brought three coffees and a tea and dealt them around the table, even though no one could yet be seen headed toward that table.

She took the saucers out from beneath each cup and placed them on top as a lid to keep the heat in a bit longer. Then, remembering something, she added another coffee before heading back in response to the *Ding!* from the kitchen indicating that someone's eggs were ready.

When she got a chance to look toward number 14 again she saw Ashton Hartock from accounts receivable hanging up his coat. The old guy was scratching his head and looking at the place settings as though he'd never seen one before. Terry called across to him.

"Happy Monday, Ashton." She got ready for shtick.

"Good morning, Terry dear! How *are* you?" He paused for her response, which she gave him in the form of a sweet smile. "So, tell me darling, what's all this?"

What a character. Ashton Hartock was a 61-year-old African-American from the Ironbound section of Newark who affected a perfect Lower East Side New York Yiddish accent. Always. Terry had never heard him speak otherwise, and so far as she knew, no one else had either. He kept it up so consistently, so innocently, that you hardly noticed anymore. That was just how he spoke. Maybe Ashton wasn't black, only looked that way. Terry had known black Jews, but they had spoken and behaved like normal black people. Ashton was unique. Maybe the routine was not an affectation at all, but just a habit. Once, years ago, Ernie had brought his mother into the office to see the place. Ashton had taken old Mrs. Lehrer on the tour. The conversation between the elderly Jewish lady and the middle aged Black man sounded, probably, just like a conversation among her friends over a *mah jongg* game on the terrace of the beachfront apartment that Ernie had bought for her in Miami. Ashton even injected Yiddish words into the conversation. Seamlessly.

"It's coffee, Ashton. It's the B Team's coffee."

"Yes. But, so much, so many?"

"Well, isn't your friend George coming back from vacation today?"

Hartock smacked his forehead and picked a chair with his back to the window. "So he is. Such a smart girl she is." He smiled at her.

Terry nodded. "And wait until Beckerhead gets in. We've had two weeks to get used to this. He's not going to know what hit him." This was Allen Kamins, wearing his *Lethal Weapon III* leather jacket. Kamins was assistant manager of the New Jersey sales department, and not one of Terry's favorites, although she couldn't quite say why.

Right behind Kamins, the remainder of the B Team appeared in short order. Ellen Cubbage, the editor of the magazines, waved to Terry.

"Have a nice weekend, Lunceford? Hello, Hartock. Kamins." Ellen called everyone by his or her last name. If everybody had to have their own thing, their trademark, Terry figured this is the one Ellen had opted for. It was like Homer Simpson's "D'oh!" Next was Hock Wasef from purchasing, who always brought both the *Daily News* and the *Post*. Finally George Becker walked in amid loud shouts of "Welcome home!" and "How was France?" and "What did you bring us?"

George looked relaxed. Terry actually felt a little sorry for this guy, despite the fact that he made three times what she made. (Lots of people at Stellar *claimed* to know what other people earned. Terry's acumen with their computer system enabled her to *actually* know. It was a mixed blessing at best.) She felt sorry for him because she figured he had yet to go through the roller coaster of emotions that she and everyone else had already experienced, and in a few minutes he would. As soon as he found out.

Unless he already knew. He probably already knew.

The conversation at the round table was more animated than the typical Monday B Team breakfast meeting. The B Team, an informal agglomeration of Stellar upper management, sometimes augmented by honorary Team members like Walter Spargo, the Venture Media rep or Robin Colasurdo, the Columbia rep, always had breakfast before work on Monday mornings at the Ultimate, for longer than Terry could remember. Non-Stellar people were occasionally allowed to join in, Terry figured, because they would always pick up the tab for the table. Terry was a woman with a vital and vivid imagination, but one thing she could not envision was what it would feel like to have an expense account.

They called themselves the B Team because they were all department heads, or managers, or assistant managers, but they weren't Ernie or Bert or Lydia, the chief of operations, or David Olean, the chief financial officer, or Tina Weiner, the head of the Jersey sales department. Those five ate lunch together most days. They didn't know it, but just because the B Team called themselves the B Team, everyone naturally referred to *them* as the A Team.

Terry wasn't surprised that George's vacation stories were not the focus of the B Team's agenda. He looked incredulous at first, but she watched as she went about her business while he slowly accepted the fact that they were not pulling his leg.

She made her way back to the table to take their orders, but they ignored her at first in the flurry of their conversation and she didn't interrupt them.

"Where are they?" George said.

"What do you mean, 'Where are they?'" Cubbage said, in her normal, gently mocking tone. "They're *gone*, George."

Kamins' tone was consistently sarcastic, never gently so. "Why, are you worried about them? They gathered up their millions, dumped the money bags with dollar signs printed on them into the trunks of their Lexuses, and drove away. To their palaces."

"No, I'm not worried about them," George said. "I – I guess I'm just getting used to this. It's kind of unreal. So what's in their offices?"

Bert and Ernie's offices were world-renowned, as famous as their former residents. For one thing, those two spacious offices, joined by a passageway with a wet bar, a little kitchen, and a bathroom with a shower, had been the scene of some of the most amazing – one might say ruthless, or perhaps some even more colorful adjectives – wheeling and dealing in the home entertainment or any other industry. On Bert's walls, in addition to family photos and pictures, some signed, some not, of him with two dozen different movie stars, one president of the United States, and three different Playboy Playmates of the Year, there also hung an original Leroy Niemann oil painting. Niemann was famous for his huge, action-oriented paintings of sports scenes and famous athletes and celebrities. Bert's Niemann, not generally known among art dealers who catalogued such things, depicted several recognizable NBA stars and at least a dozen nude young women, in and around a large hot tub. Ernie's office was less overtly sexual but just as expensively appointed.

"Get it straight, Becker. There's nothing in those offices now. The desks, the chairs, the shelves. A few boxes," Cubbage said.

"The king is dead," Hock said. "The kings are dead. Long live the king."

"What are they going to do?"

Ashton spoke up. "George, you are truly a beautiful human being," he said. "You are asking the very same questions that occurred to all of us in the last week or two. From what I hear, they signed a non-compete clause. They can not work in or start any business related in any way to video, or any other kind of software or entertainment."

"Wow." George truly seemed amazed. "Why would they agree to such a thing?"

"Don't you get it? I've never known you to be naïve." Kamins had a way of saying things that from someone else might sound neutral, or mildly complimentary, but from him sounded insulting. "For MONEY, baby. Lots of it. The twenty or thirty million bucks they split between them – depending on who you believe – was just the beginning. Now they're both gonna get paid their outrageous salaries every two weeks for the next two years, while they visit their various homes and spoil their jug-headed, misbegotten grandchildren."

George was starting to get it, but he still looked a little bewildered. Ellen Cubbage leaned over and rubbed George's shoulder in a patronizing manner. "Becker. Get used to it. It's a new day. And before it's over, we're all gonna get fucked."

Terry remained transfixed, until Ashton said, "Well, we still have to eat. You gotta eat every day. Shall we order?" But before he asked for his over easy eggs he looked over at Cubbage. "Ellen, you're a nice girl, but, *oy*, that's some mouth you got on you. I mean, you're right, of course, but still..."

TERRY COULDN'T PAY TOO MUCH ATTENTION TO THE B Team. It wasn't even really her table, though she and Kelly and the other girls often swapped tables as it suited them. She got busy with her other customers and let Kelly bring the B Team their orders. Now it had gotten busy, and the next time she looked over she saw the Stellar people leaving.

Terry wouldn't get to her desk for another few hours. When the breakfast rush was finally over she would change her clothes and take the half hour break she allowed herself before she switched to her other role. Working two jobs wasn't as hard as it sounded, although if people wanted to cut her some slack on account of it, she let them. It was no picnic either. She worked from 11 until six in the evening, in the credit department. (Ironic, she always felt, since her own credit was so often a shambles. The customers she had to call to remind them – nicely, if she could; more forcefully, if nice didn't work – to pay their bills would never know that though.) The good part was that Ernie had made a deal with her when he heard what her whole situation was, allowing her a long lunch in the middle of the afternoon. With that she was able to go to Bayonne and pick Sammy up at school, take him home, eat with him, start him on his homework. Ernie probably didn't know how important this was for Terry, or for Sammy. Or who knows? Maybe he did.

Terry hadn't gotten a raise last March, when she was due. Not that she was singled out; everyone's increases had been postponed for three months, because Stellar had lost a couple of big customers, and things were just a little rocky for a time. But Terry had made out anyway. One night when Bert had been working late, he stopped at her desk to chat. He saw on her desk the *Star-Ledger* classified section.

"You lookin' for a new job?" the boss wanted to know.

"If I wanted a new job, would I be checking the ads while sitting at my desk at work?"

Bert had laughed at that one. He seemed to like the fact that everyone at Stellar had a pretty relaxed relationship. You didn't have to show him all kinds of deference. Usually. "What kind of car?"

"The kind I can afford, which is at this point is probably a used piece of shit hoopty with one of the doors tied on with rope."

A few evenings later, Bert called Terry into that big office. He was sorry she'd had to go without a raise. Then, to her amazement, he gave her the Subaru. His son had been using it while he was in charge of sales for their video game division. Video games had not gone well for Stellar, Dougie had decided to take an extended vacation in Europe, and the car was just sitting there. Could Terry use it? You bet she could.

Terry was really quite moved at this. His only request was that they keep it between them. He'd tell Ernie, of course, but no one else was to know about their deal. They'd say she had bought it and leave it at that. She went around his desk and gave him a hug. She couldn't help herself. Of course, Bert had to ruin it by grabbing her ass and kissing her neck. She had extricated herself easily, and punched him in the chest. But not too hard. Feminist Terry clucked at Real World Terry who found she couldn't really stay mad at him. The next day, an interoffice envelope was on her desk with the Subaru's pink slip inside and the key.

Chapter Four
Life in the Fast Lane,
Surely Make You Lose Your...

1997

HE TOOK A SMALL HIT, NOT HIS FIRST, OFF THE FAT joint clenched between his fingertips. To Lane Coutell, it all made sense. It fit, like the soft, satisfying *thunk!* the door of his new Beemer made when he shut it. No wait, wait. It fit... it fit like the tumblers of a lock whose combination he'd been trying to break for two decades. Yeah, this was destiny working here baby!

Oh, he'd paid his dues, that was for sure. He'd knocked himself out for Bert and Ernie, especially in the early years. Hell, he'd married Bert's daughter Johanna in the early eighties. Granted it only lasted eighteen-and-a-half days. Eighteen-and-a-half frightening (another puff) days. But Lane had learned from that, and everything that didn't kill Lane made him stronger. That's what the crystal paperweight on his new desk had engraved on it. His girlfriend Kristy gave it to him for his new office, in honor of his ascension to the presidency. And it was not just a paperweight. It was a paperweight *and* a business card holder. And that was important, maybe the most important office furnish*ing* – as opposed to furni*ture* – in his whole new set up. Because when people came to see him, now, in Ernie's old office, their eyes would be drawn to Lane's new business cards. The ones that said "President" on them. No "Vice" anymore. Hell, what did "Vice" even mean, anyway? (Puff, puff.) It wasn't vice like the vice squad. It wasn't vice like that squeezy thing on a tool bench. Now that he really thought about it, Vice President was a stupid title, and he was glad he would never have to be called that again.

Anyone could be a vice president. Not everyone could be a president. That's what made America great. And that's what made Lane Coutell great.

Lane's silver Beemer was blasting down the New York State Thruway at over 90 miles an hour, the radar detector beeping its all clear signal at two am. Just like Lane's future: All clear sailing from here on, baby. He zoomed past the sign that said "EXIT 18, SUNY NEW PALTZ, 2 MILES." He knew this exit all too well. He had a sudden impulse to get off at Exit 18, to go to New Paltz. How much fun would that be, to go there, right now, on the spur of the moment, and show those fuckers. Ha! And then, the more he thought about it, the more it grew from a crazy thought to a realistic plan: *Sure, why not?* He'd pull right up to the Radical Radish or the Perverted Penguin or wherever the fuck they all hung out now. His would be the only Beemer in the parking lot, that was for damn sure! Chicks would come around. All the people who'd patronized him, who had looked down at him during the three semesters he'd gone there, their fucking jaws would fall open. *FUCK THEM! I'M THE BOSS. I'M IN THE DRIVER'S SEAT. I'M THE GOD DAMNED PRESIDENT!*

Lane actually slowed the new car down to 70 and slid over into the right lane in preparation for taking the exit as he had done so many times before, so long ago. But he realized, just in time, that it was the middle of the night, and that in all likelihood none of the same kids would still be there that he'd known in the 1970s, so he didn't actually take the exit. Instead he revved it up over 100. He was alone on the road, but he seemed to see himself from above and somewhere to the right, as though there were a camera on a boom, or a helicopter, tracking him, filming him, revealing Lane Coutell in this, what felt like his victory lap. The first of many victory laps to come. It was a glorious feeling, triumphant, and it needed a soundtrack. He punched the Bang & Olufsen and, as if God Himself had planned it, there it was: Blue Oyster Cult, "Don't Fear the Reaper." YEAH! That's right! President Lane Coutell didn't fear the God damned Reaper.

He cranked that sucker up and sang along.

> *Laa, la LA la LA la LA!*
> *Laa, la LA la LA la LA!*
> *Come on baby, don't fear the Reaper!*
> *Come and take my hand, don't fear the Reaper!*[1]

Lane punched the button that automatically floated all the windows down, and cranked the volume two more notches. He tried to take one more hit, but the wind sucked the roach right out of his fingernails. *Who cares? Plenty more where that came from.* If anyone were awake in New Paltz, indeed if anyone was awake anywhere in Sullivan County, they'd hear him and BOC roaring through, roaring past them. Leaving them in his dust.

The wind was exhilarating!

> *We'll be able to fly, don't fear the Reaper!*
> *Baby I'M YOUR MAN!!!!*[1]

The wind was too much. It sucked Lane's toupee up, back, around the side of his head, and out the window. He didn't slow down.

Chapter Five
What This Country Really Needs

1975

THE NOISE LEVEL WAS DEAFENING, BUT IF HE HAD learned anything in five years of teaching at Monmouth County Regional Junior High School, he had learned to almost completely ignore the shrill, mind-boggling cacophony of the cafeteria. (*Hey, that was not bad, "shrill, mind-boggling cacophony."* He pulled a small notebook from his jacket's inner pocket and wrote it down. In Sixth Period Creative Writing they were working on colorful, sensory descriptions, and he was trying to keep it interesting.) This was lunch duty, and there wasn't a damn thing anybody could do about the noise. Any lunch period where no fight broke out and nothing heavier than a grape or deadlier than a pizza crust got hurled at anyone was an unqualified success.

One of the few things a teacher on lunch duty was required to do without fail was to prevent the export of foodstuffs to other parts of the building. Mr. Becker's Lunch Duty partner today was Vice Principal Sylvia Mumminger. The two had deployed themselves as follows: First twenty minutes of lunch,

Becker in the main doorway leading into the school's front lobby, stopping cookie smugglers and sneaky people with apple juice or tuna fish under their jackets; Mumminger roaming among the tables, trying to keep peace. Second half, switch. Becker preferred roaming, talking to the kids, greeting this one, teasing that one. Doorway sucked; it was even more boring and he hated to stand still, so he was glad when the clock ticked past 12:31 and he and the Vice Principal switched.

As he roamed, he saw his pal, Ward Kercy, the eighth grade social studies teacher and girls' soccer coach. Ward popped out of the teachers' cafeteria and caught his eye.

"George, I gotta talk to you about something."

"OK. What?"

"An idea. No, not here. Later."

"Fine by me. Very mysterious. Later when and where?"

"Can you meet me at The Swamp, after soccer practice?"

"Say five o'clock? That's fine."

Becker wondered what could be such a big deal that they couldn't talk about it in the midst of all this screaming. Regardless, he probably would have hit their favorite after-work bar later anyway, affectionately nicknamed after the aroma it sometimes gave off, particularly on Sundays after a football game.

Becker kept roaming as Kercy headed with his empty tray toward the trash barrels. George saw a kid stand up and take a full wind-up, in preparation for chucking a muffin across the cafeteria. Fortunately, the kid, Jesse Calabrese, a ninth grader, didn't see Ward passing behind him. Ward simply plucked the muffin, still wrapped in plastic, right out of the kid's hand at the top of his wind up, pocketed it, and kept going as if the muffin had been slipped to him by an invisible courier. George laughed out loud. Ward was good like that. And the other kids at the table were now laughing at Jesse, who had begun his release before realizing he had no more muffin. One of the kids pointed at Jesse and called, "Balk!"

George roamed around near the door, and as he did so he

noticed Andre "Peanut Head" Brautigan strolling amiably toward the door, on his way outside. Andre was peeling a banana as he walked. Bananas were, of course, an ideal food to NOT allow out of the cafeteria, and Becker wanted to see how Sylvia would handle it. This vice-principal was not renowned for her mastery of discipline. No. If he was going to demand accuracy of his students' writing and thinking, he should employ it himself. V.P. Mumminger was a world-class pushover. If you had to throw a kid out of your class and send him to the office, it would do you no good if he wound up speaking to Ms. Mumminger. He'd just miss the rest of your class, and rarely if ever get any punishment. Sometimes she would have the kid "work" for a couple of periods in the office, run some errands for her, effectively allowing him to miss several classes, and reinforcing his belief that he could mouth off to whatever teacher had sent him down there. It could be said that Ms. Mumminger was worse than a pushover; she was an enabler, and everybody knew it.

As he crossed the threshold, Ms. Mumminger called, in her conciliatory voice, "Excuse me? Peanut?"

Peanut was swallowing the first bite of his banana. He didn't slow his already languid pace, nor did he turn his head to look at her. He peeled it a little further and said, "What banana? I ain't got no banana." And he continued to peel it as he walked outside, unmolested.

R EMEMBER LAST YEAR, WHEN WE RENTED *LAWRENCE of Arabia* and took the kids to the Regency for a field trip to see it?"

"Yeah, of course I remember."

"Ok. Now, remember earlier this year, when you and I went to that porno theater in New York and saw *Deep Throat* and *Behind the Green Door*?"

"In great detail, yes, I remember that quite well."

Ward sat back a little, took a deep swig of his beer, and let a little satisfied look play across his craggy features. George didn't get it. But this was typical of many conversations he'd had with Ward. No one knew exactly how old Ward was, but George guessed that he was somewhere between fifty-five and sixty. Some thought he was well preserved and much older. Others thought he was only forty, and looked much older because he had gone through so much hell in his life. Ward would never cop to his age, but he clearly enjoyed doling out fatherly-type advice to the younger guys he hung out with on the faculty. His style, used both in his classroom and out of it, was overly pedantic; he would give you bits of the information, see if you could guess where he was going, then a few more bits, and then more, until he'd bring you to some conclusion that he could very well have told you in the beginning, without all the background. It was the Socratic method, Jersey shore-style. The younger guys could afford to cut Ward some slack. He never bad-mouthed either of his exes, and he often spoke proudly about his kids. All George knew was that of the tough experiences in Ward's life, he ranked his stay in a POW camp during the Korean War *third*.

"What do those two things have in common, George, my lad?" Ward signaled Patty behind the bar that they were ready for a couple more beers.

George thought for a moment. "Well, they both involved movies. And movie theaters."

"OK. Good."

"Very different kinds of movies."

"You don't miss a trick, George. Now, what else did those two fine cinematic experiences have in common?"

George could not for the life of him guess where this was going, but he'd find out soon, because he knew that Ward needed to get to Sears out at the mall to sell appliances at six-thirty. What *did* they have in common? Popcorn? Certainly not the audience or the quality of the stories.

"Help me out here, oh wise guru," George said.

"Well, first of all, these were not first-run films."

"OK. Excuse me, but so the fuck what?"

"Patience, grasshopper. Listen and learn." Ward took another sip, downed a shot of something clear that Patty had delivered to accompany their beers, and then another sip of beer, before he finally continued. "Both showings were for specific types of audiences, for specific purposes. *Lawrence of Arabia* we had Tommy order special, arranged a special private showing at his theater, and showed it to the kids in support of stuff that both of us are teaching in our classes. The porn flicks also have a unique, but different, purpose for the audience, mostly but not all male, who watched it. You with me?"

"Yeah, but I don't see where– "

"What's the one drawback of going to the movie theater to see dirty movies?"

This one George knew. "Well, it was the best quality porn I've ever seen, not that I've seen so much, and on a bigger screen than those stag films we got for Simon's bachelor party. But I guess the real drawback is that guys like me and you, we're just not the raincoat-and-newspaper type."

"Meaning?"

"Meaning that at a certain point, you kinda wish there weren't any people around while you're getting a hard-on watching naked chicks do outrageous things."

"You'd rather be alone. Like, say, in your apartment."

"Yeah, but– "

"Now what was most unique about watching *Lawrence?* That we were able to tell them when to start the film, and to stop at key points so we could have a discussion making sure the kids were getting it all, then tell them to start it again, all at our convenience?"

"Um, All of the Above?"

"Bingo. What if you could do that with porno movies?"

"Take our students to see them and have an intermission in the middle to make sure they were understanding everything?"

"No, putz. OK look, here's what I'm talking about. I know this guy. Szimansky. A lawyer. Don't ask me how I know him.

OK, he's my first ex-wife's second ex-husband, if you must know. So sometimes we talk to each other, because we have both suffered the same – never mind, all that's beside the point. The point is Szimansky works for one of the big Hollywood movie studios, Twentieth Century Fox. Specifically, he's in charge of writing contracts for what they call 'ancillary rights.' That means everything other than regular theatrical distribution, like when they sell a movie to TV, when they sell it to distributors overseas, soundtrack albums, books about the movies, all that kind of shit.

"So Szimansky had to draw up a new kind of contract the other day. He told me that some guy from Ohio or Nevada or somewhere is purchasing the right to take a whole bunch of Twentieth Century Fox's best movies, like *Patton*, and *The Sound of Music*, and *M*A*S*H*, and *The African Queen*, and *The Longest Day*, and sell copies of them that people can watch at home."

"Well how big a market could there be of people who have movie theaters in their homes?"

"That's where it gets more interesting. They're not going to be on film. They're going to be transferred to video tape."

"Yeah, but still..."

"And there's a new machine that's recently come on the market, that shmucks like you and me don't know about – yet. Sony makes it. It's called a Betamax. Now these Betamax machines cost like fifteen hundred or two thousand bucks. And what they are, they're tape cassette players – for *video* tape. Just like your cassette deck plays music cassettes through your stereo amplifier and your speakers, these Betamax video cassettes play in a Betamax machine, which is plugged into your TV, and you can watch what's on 'em. You can hit pause so you can go to the bathroom or go get something to eat."

"You can hit rewind and go back over a part that you like or if you didn't get it." George was starting to get it.

"No commercials."

"No commercials?"

"No commercials. And unlike food and rent and alimony

and college tuition, electronic things get *cheaper* as they become more popular. An automatic icemaker on a Sears freezer used to add $300 to the cost of the appliance. Now I can sell you one where the icemaker is on the outside so you don't even have to open the freaking door. And it only adds about $110 bucks to the price of the freezer. These Betamaxes could cost $350-400 bucks in two years, if there are movies for people to put into them. And if more and more contracts like the one Szymanski wrote last week get written, and I think they will, then people everywhere are going to be watching movies at home. In fact, lots of people *already* are watching movies at home. You know how I know? I got into a conversation with the owner of that porno theater in the city. Yeah, I've been back there, shut up, that ain't the point. Somebody came to him and asked his permission to put a rack of these Betamax movie cassette thingies in the theater lobby. All porno movies, only this guy called them "adult movies." All of them, according to the guy, ten times filthier than *Deep Throat*. And this guy just wanted him to leave the rack there, offer them for sale for sixty bucks each, and they'd split the money fifty-fifty.

"Now the theater owner thought the guy was a moron, and he didn't think anything would happen, but the guy with these Betamax movies was persistent, and so finally to shut him up he let him do it. Guess what happened? No, don't guess, I'll tell you. All seventy-two tapes sold out in four days.

"Now you think about this, because I gotta go to work. We'll talk more tomorrow." Ward dropped some money on the bar, winked at George, and left.

Why was Ward telling him this stuff? What was "the idea" that they'd met here to discuss, in private, lest someone else overhear? Ward always had his ear to the ground for "the next big thing" because, he believed, those who knew the next big thing before everybody else were the ones who got rich and didn't have to work two and three jobs just to afford to live and support a family… or, in his case, families. But what did he think was gonna happen? Were he and George going to pool their funds and invest in Sony stock? Ha. They wouldn't be able to buy more than a share or two. Did he think that George and he would set up shop on the boardwalk, or walk up and down the beach hawking movies? Get your *Patton*, right here! I got Julie Andrews, who needs *Sound of Music*?!

George smiled at the mental picture he'd just painted. He finished his beer and left. He had a date.

FOUR HOURS LATER, GEORGE SAT UP IN ALICE MAY'S bed. Alice May had been his official girlfriend for a couple of months now. He didn't know how he was this lucky, but he sure wasn't questioning it. Alice May Buford was a southern belle transplanted to New Jersey, but she didn't fit the southern belle stereotype. She was an associate professor of ancient history at nearby Monmouth College. She had a Ph. D. in anthropology. Three years older than George, she was the most beautiful thing he had ever seen.

She was, in fact, a classic. A shy girl with a body like Marilyn Monroe, a face like the Greek statue of Aphrodite he'd shown the kids at the Metropolitan Museum of Art, hair like a chocolate waterfall, she had an unholy sex drive which she said George discovered and unleashed. George wasn't used to women telling him stuff like that, and he wasn't used to sleeping with women who looked like beauty queens. But this one did, and he really, really liked it.

Exquisite, naked and smiling dreamily, Alice May was enjoying a warm afterglow nap, using George's bare thigh for a pillow. In a couple of minutes, George would disturb her sleep to begin again, and Alice May would awake with an amazed and appreciative squeal of delight. But for once, for this minute in between, that's not what he was thinking about. At this particular moment he was thinking about movies in little plastic boxes. Millions and millions of them.

Chapter Six
Spare Change

1997

THE NEXT THREE MONTHS AT STELLAR UNSPOOLED IN a blur of newness. At first, it all seemed unreal to Terry. Change so fundamental as this, as Bert and Ernie transitioning from institution status to remembered symbols of a time gone by, icons of nostalgia instead of forces to be feared as well as reckoned with. It just didn't seem that kind of change could possibly take place without explosions, earthquakes, gunfire, mayhem. Their offices, for example – no matter who occupied them, wouldn't they always be referred to as Bert's or Ernie's office? She thought of "Bunny's desk" in the accounting department where they kept the coffeepot and a constantly replenished supply of home made baked goods. Bunny had been an accounts payables person for a little over a year before she got canned, along with a new receptionist. It was literally the new receptionist's first day on the job, which explains why no one could remember her name or too much about her other than that she was almost six feet tall and had a Jamaican accent. They were fired when Lydia, who seemed to have a sort of primitive instinct for ferreting out this sort of thing, came upon the two of them in the upstairs file room. Lydia was quoted by several people as saying that "the two of them were butt naked" and that Bunny was climbing that Jamaican girl like a tree" and "using her like a ride at Coney Island." The two women had been so lost in each other that Lydia had gotten quite a tutorial in "how lesbos do it," as she'd reported later. But that had happened four years ago. If everyone still called accounting's coffee spot "Bunny's desk," wouldn't the two big, notorious offices of the bosses always be "Bert & Ernie's offices?"

But the forces of change have no respect for the past or for people's ingrained habits. Terry wasn't surprised when Lane Coutell from Massachusetts was installed as "the president of Stellar" which was now "the video division of Circular Records." He'd moved into Ernie's office and, remarkably, had quickly made it his own. Lane owned a lot of movie memorabilia, including a life-sized Imperial storm trooper from *Star Wars* which was now the first thing you noticed when you walked into that room. The second thing was Lane's collection of autographed baseball caps. There must be some kind of law that movie directors in Hollywood, while shooting new movies, had to wear baseball caps bearing the logo of the movie they were shooting, and Lane had managed to get a constant flow of these caps, autographed by their former owners, and had tacked them in a row all along the wall of the office. It no longer looked like Ernie's office. It was Lane's office.

Bert's former office was now the "guest office," meaning that when hotshots from California came to Jersey City, they'd go in there to work. The door to that office was almost always closed now, whether or not a Circular exec was in residence. In the old days, about the only time Bert's office door was shut was when he was doing something that he shouldn't be doing. Judy Frink, who sat outside both of the bosses' offices and who was no fool, acted as their guard dog, simply shaking her head if somebody came down to visit Bert when he was "otherwise engaged." When Bert eventually emerged from his office in a disgustingly cheerful mood, he would take Judy Frink to the lunch room and buy her a Twix or a Dr. Pepper. That was when the young woman – always a very young woman – who had been meeting with Bert would have the opportunity to slip out and return to whatever she was supposed to be doing. The whole procedure was one of several of the worst kept secrets in the office.

But now, when one of the Circular people was sitting at Bert's old desk, the door was frequently closed. Sometimes, the door to the passageway between the two offices would also be closed, which would always make Lane nervous as hell. In fact, Terry noticed that Lane, thought of up until then as a happy-go-lucky sort of guy, was really nervous whenever one of the people from California was there. He answered his phone before the first ring died out. He reorganized all the items on his desk top unnecessarily, compulsively, daily. He now kept a bottle of Mylanta in his desk, and sipped from it regularly.

Sometimes Brian Fallow or Peter Ng or Angela Crofut or one of the others would visit, and Lane would pick them up at Newark, no matter what time they arrived, and drive them to the office. (For reasons she could not fathom, it had recently become one of Terry's new duties to book flights for executives. Other than the way the job had mysteriously and unceremoniously just *become* hers one day, she didn't totally mind this, because it wasn't hard, and it gave her an interesting insight into the comings and goings of the people who clearly were planning all of their destinies.) They would walk into Bert's old office, greeting warmly each person they passed on the way in, as if they were old buddies. Then they'd close the door behind them, sometimes not come out all day, even for lunch. They could spend a whole week there and rarely step outside that office. *Why the hell did they need to be in Jersey City to sit inside an office all day? Didn't they have their own offices in Davis? Why fly all the way across the country to be in the "headquarters" of the "video division," and barely communicate with any of the video people who were there? What was the point?* It made Terry a little uncomfortable when she couldn't figure out people's motivations, because usually she was pretty good at it.

But if she was a bit put out, Lane was completely freaked. Normally Lane spent most of his day working on his computer. She knew from her conversations with some of the people who worked in Stockbridge that Lane spent a good portion of his day downloading and staring at porn from the Internet. The visiting studio reps frequently gave him pornographic computer games in exchange for him yelling at the salespeople to sell those reps' titles. Lane had ordered a new computer the day he'd arrived in Jersey City, a computer "suitable for a president," he'd told her, with a huge screen, and more speed and memory than anyone else's in the building. Amazing, considering the fact that he possibly did less work on his new computer while spending more money buying it and more time using it than anyone else did on their inferior machines. She could tell that he had largely curtailed his extra-curricular computer usage lately. At first he didn't give a crap if she or anyone else noticed something on his screen that was obviously not work-related. These days he'd go out of his way in a failed attempt to appear cool as he cleared his screen whenever anybody came in. As if he'd been staring so intently at a blank screen that he had barely noticed that someone had entered.

If nothing else, Circular was all about new technology. The bright billion-dollar future of this new combined entity was based in large part on what was coming around the corner like a locomotive: the Internet revolution. *Hitch your caboose to this train,* it was said, *do whatever it takes to feed the Internet beast, and the sky would be the limit. For the foreseeable future.* Terry recognized that she was mixing metaphors maniacally, a thing she normally hated to do even in her head, but it didn't matter. *Go! Go! Go!* If you were a supplier to Internet retailers, like this new bookstore on the web called Amazon Dot Com, you were gonna get rich. And then you were gonna get richer. She didn't know what books had to do with a river in Brazil, but she had read the stories about how everyone at Microsoft, even the secretaries, became millionaires – management, of course, became gazillionaires, but still – retired at 43 with their stock options, and became philanthropists. Terry wasn't exactly sure what stock options were, but she sure hoped that she'd get some in this new world order. Maybe she wouldn't get to be a millionaire, but maybe she'd score something for herself and Sammy and Mama before it all came crashing down.

Probably not though.

And it was sure to come crashing down. She didn't need to be a financial wizard or read the *Wall Street Journal* to know that. She felt it.

BOOKING FLIGHTS FOR THE HOTSHOTS WAS NOT THE only new responsibility that Terry had recently acquired in what many people had taken to calling the New World Order. Something else had come her way which wound up putting her right in the middle of lots of top level meetings. As with the travel booking, while she wasn't exactly thrilled, some part of her felt, well, *flattered* when she was given new responsibilities. And she also liked it when she was privy to inside information. Both of these things made her feel a little bit safer.

The last time Brian Fallow had come to Jersey City, he'd had a meeting with all the Stellar department heads. Unlike anything Bert or Ernie had ever done, whenever Brian Fallow had a meeting, someone other than one of the participants in the meeting needed to take notes. Minutes. It should have been Judy Frink's job, but Judy was on vacation. Maybe because she was doing an acceptable job with his travel, or maybe because she was the only other person whose name he knew who was not a manager, Terry was asked to take notes at this meeting. So she was right there and knew all about it.

That first meeting at which she took the minutes turned out to be a lulu. It was when the Stellarites found out that they were about to reap the nearly unlimited benefits of teleconferencing.

On her notepad, under the date and the list of first names of the people in the room, Terry wrote: *Teleconferencing.*

"What do we need it for?" was the initial response, voiced by Lydia, but expressing what had occurred to Terry as well as most of the others in the room, no doubt, after Fallow informed them that he was having teleconferencing equipment installed in Jersey City, Stockbridge, Cincinnati, Minneapolis and, of course, Davis. "What's it gonna cost?"

Terry wrote: *Cost? Purpose?*

"Uh, excuse me honey," interjected Tina, "Before we get to that, just what the f– What is teleconferation, or whatever it is? What's it for? It sounds confusing. I don't think I'm gonna like it."

"Excellent first questions!" Fallow smiled his patient smile which Terry had already learned contained nine parts condescension for each part of actual empathy. "I love how everyone here takes the practical approach, cuts to the most essential issues first."

"It's how we've been brought up," said Allen Kamins drily.

To the amazement of everyone in the room, by way of explanation, Fallow put a promotional video from the teleconferencing equipment company into the VCR, and they all watched a five-minute tour of the benefits of teleconferencing. Terry sat at the far end of the table from the screen, alongside Fallow, so she could see the back of everyone's heads as they all watched. Even from that vantage, their body language told her that there was a great deal of eye rolling among the group.

"Better be careful," Kamins stage-whispered to the advertising manager, Stacy Piatti. "They say the camera puts on ten pounds."

Kamins was sitting in front of Stacy, which made it easy for her to slap the back of his head, while the others snickered. "I can lose weight, but you can't lose stupid," she retorted, and got a bigger laugh. Fallow made a half-hearted attempt to join in the friendly, familiar banter, but he clearly was uncomfortable doing it. Terry had a sudden image flash through her head, of a rich family of skinny, pointy-nosed WASPS, sitting around a large dinner table, quietly, coldly, stiffly. Uncomfortable. Smiles in place, but with dead eyes. She shook it off.

The jokes continued, but Terry felt that there was a nervous self-consciousness to it. These people knew each other very well, they were used to each other's quirks, like Kamins' obligatory put-downs and Tina's ubiquitous "honey," which she applied to everyone she addressed, regardless of gender or how long she'd known the person. There was not the usual ease in the room, and the reason was obvious. First of all, this was their first managers' meeting with Fallow, their first official post-B&E meeting. Secondly, these were the people who for several years had been making many of the important decisions at Stellar. Bert and Ernie were, of course, the final arbiters of everything at Stellar – up until two weeks ago, that is – but new equipment, different computers, changes in how things were done had, generally, been initiated by the people in this room. It had been a long time since they were called into a room and told, "This is what we're going to do," about anything significant. More than teleconferencing, this would be the hardest thing for these people to get used to. It might, in fact, be impossible for some of them.

The video explained that teleconferencing was the communication wave of the future. With cameras and TVs in all your locations, a company could save hundreds of thousands in airfare and other travel expenses, meetings could take place more easily, consultation between decision-makers on opposite sides of the country would be facilitated. The actors in the video, portraying a carefully-diverse, power-suited array of male and female executives, wore self-confident smiles, and seemed deeply satisfied with the ease with which they accomplished their missions by means of teleconferencing. A sales exec in New York City had a heart-to-heart with his top road warrior about to call on a big customer in Memphis. A marketing group in L.A. made an interactive presentation with a team from their top client's office in Seattle, and everyone in both rooms spoke up and asked each other questions as if they were all in one room. This technology even allowed people to talk (and visualize!) each other in five different locations at once, with split screens. It all seemed like something they'd all seen before – on *Star Trek*.

The tape ended, Hock flipped the lights back on, and Lydia said, "What do we need it for? What's it gonna cost?" By maintaining the precise tone she had used earlier, she conveyed that the video had not inspired her.

Fallow wasn't intimidated in the least. "I can't give you the final figure yet, but it will be in the neighborhood of two hundred seventy-five to three hundred thousand."

Several people made little "holy shit" sounds. Fallow ignored them.

Terry wrote: *equipment cost: approx. $300K* on her note pad.

"And what we need it for is this. We are in the first stage of a very difficult endeavor. Does anybody know what that is?" The question was clearly rhetorical.

"We're trying to make one big company out of two smaller ones. You may think that when the deal was signed by the owners on both sides, then we had one larger company. Nothing could be further from the truth. That was the prelude to the hard work. The hard work, the *real* work starts now.

"It won't be as hard as crossing a dog and a cat. But that's almost like what we have to do." He stood up, and warmed to his topic. It was obvious he'd already given this talk, maybe in different form, in another room with a different, more receptive audience. "Sure, both Stellar and Circular are wholesalers of entertainment software that gets sold through retailers to consumers, who take it home and watch or listen to it. But in so many ways, our companies are very different."

Terry's pen hovered uncertainly over her page, so she was relieved when he looked to his left and said, "There's no need for you to take notes on this part, Terry. Or any of you. But please listen, because it's so important for me to get this across to you. We have different ways of selling, different ways of shipping, different ways of billing. Our customer bases overlap 9%; that's the good news. That means that they are 91% different from each other. That's how much potential new business each group gets, right off the bat. But it will be a challenge. Picking up that business is not a low-hanging fruit.

"We have different salary scales, different computer systems, different phone systems, different organizational plans, different histories. The average age of non-management employees at Circular Records is twenty-three. The average age of non-management employees at Stellar Video is thirty-three.

"The best way to describe this, the way management consultants put it, is that we have to take two entirely different cultures and change them into one."

"Not to worry, we have no culture at all here," joked Ellen Cubbage.

No one so much as chuckled, and Fallow hardly paused in his speech to indicate to Ellen, with only the briefest look in her direction, that now he was not interested in improvisational comedy. "If this acquisition had not happened, it would be a safe bet that Stellar would have gone out of business within two years." Anticipating their quick, astonished reaction, he cut them off definitively. "Trust me, I *know*. I'll be glad to show you the figures some time. Same thing for Circular. Maybe three years. Businesses like ours are ticking time bombs. But combined, there is a critical mass. In the next three years, maybe sooner, three-quarters of the video distributors currently in existence will be gone. History. Same for music. I intend for this company to be, if necessary, the last man standing. Because, if we can get past this transition phase, we will have everything in place.

"Get ready, people. We have a rosy future, an incredible future, a rich future ahead for all of us, after we get over this part. Everyone in this room is going to make a ton of money." To her astonishment he turned to look briefly but directly at Terry. "Yes, everybody." Normally she didn't like it when people practiced voodoo or read her thoughts without her permission, but she couldn't help but like what he was saying. She didn't have to believe it to take a little pleasure, even if temporary, in the concept.

"But this transition is the hardest job, the *sine qua non*, and you, and the managers at the other Stellar locations, and the Executive Council in Davis, are the ones who have to figure out how to do it. I'm not going to do it. I can't. You can, and you will.

"Some companies fail at this, and the new entity dies. This is a most dangerous time for us. We are vulnerable. If each of us in management doesn't set the right tone, and doesn't work together to get this done, then chances are we will fail.

"And I don't like to fail."

A tight, ugly little smile spread like an ink stain across his face. Terry had heard this new boss of all of theirs speak in front of groups five, maybe six times already. But this was different. His tone was different, his body language was different. It was almost as if there were two different Brian Fallowses, one who spoke in buzzwords and optimistic generalities, a cheerleader, a booster, and this other one, the one she now saw for the first time. He was a small man with a beaky sort of face, Fallow. A dark cloud had passed over his features when his tone changed. He hadn't raised his voice at all, but this beak-faced little raptor had just morphed from Big Bird to a screaming eagle.

And there wasn't a person in the room who failed to see the transformation.

Chapter Seven
What's in a Name?

1997

THINGS CHANGED; THINGS REMAINED THE SAME. David Olean left of his own accord a week after Bert and Ernie. He spent his last day sitting with various people in the office, saying his goodbyes after thirteen years. He wasn't bitter. Or, if he was, he certainly didn't show it.

"It's really simple, George. One company will not have two CFOs. It can't happen. And when they eliminate one CFO, it's not going to be the one they know. It would be me. So I'm just going to make it easier on everyone."

George liked David a lot, and he was sorry to see him go, but what he was saying made sense. "They said they'll maintain us as a separate division," he told his departing friend.

David was patient. "Remember two things. To protect yourself. First, there won't be a separate finance department for each division. That would be nuts. All those people are going to go, despite any speeches Brian has made. They have to. It's business, not personal. And ultimately, there won't be any redundancies."

"What's the other thing?"

"Look, maybe they'll keep video as a separate division. You and your department could have a future here. But this isn't the first time one company has bought another. There's a history to this, a pattern. Not that every takeover is the same, they're not. But there is one constant. They will say and do anything to make the transition successful. They pretty much have to. So if that means lying to all of these people who depend on this place for their livelihoods, who have made this place successful, then they will lie. And they'll feel justified."

"I guess you're right."

"Of course I am. And you know what else? If we had bought them, we'd be doing the same thing."

For several weeks after Olean's departure, things remained pretty stable. In reality, George was too busy to worry about company politics. Late summer was Christmas for marketing, meaning every single project, and there were hundreds of them, was in high gear, everything was either behind schedule or about to be, and Becker and everyone in his department was working long hours, even some weekends to get it all done. If Ernie was still here he would wander upstairs to marketing, a thing he rarely did because A) he trusted George, and B) it was a longer walk than he cared to take if it wasn't necessary. But on occasions like this he would come upstairs, because it pleased him to see everybody working so hard. "That's what I like to see," he'd say. "Heads down and assholes twitching."

In most years, the holiday season would make or break your whole year. Last year Stellar did as much business in the fourth quarter as they did in the first nine months of the year. And this year, the balance would tilt further. This was because Stellar had changed its strategy from what it had been in the first decade and a half of the video business. Engle, VMG, Cooke & Aster and the other competing distributors were a little slower than Bert & Ernie had been. Not that Stellar was the biggest, not at all. They ranked between fourth and sixth, depending on the time of year and who was doing the ranking. No, it was because

Stellar was smaller that they were lighter on their feet. A huge company like Engle, with interests around the world, thousands of stockholders, a board of directors, couldn't change as quickly as a company only a twentieth of their size, a company where a change in the business plan could happen in a day. All a company like that needed was a little information, and a lot of will.

Back in the eighties, Stellar was among the first to recognize that the business was evolving from the traditional rental model into a sell-through business. Cheaper videos with minuscule profit margins were going to be sold in massively bigger quantities; the mom and pop video stores were probably doomed; and the Wal-Marts and Costcos of the world would become the place where people would get their video fix.

Stellar was thriving, growing, as other distributors struggled. Several got the idea, but Stellar had a head start. And that was all they had needed. The irony, George and everyone else now realized, was that it was precisely this success that had led to the precarious situation in which they all found themselves.

All, of course, except B&E. Guesses of how much each had walked away with varied, but it was certainly eight figures each. Olean knew, he had to in his position, but he respected the confidence. Others said they knew, but they were guessing. It didn't matter. In the final analysis, B&E had taken the money and they had run, and the people who had played such an important part in getting them there were stuck with an uncertain future. Ernie had always called Stellar "a family;" many of its employees now felt like orphans abandoned into the care of a scary foster parent.

STOCKBRIDGE, ARE YOU THERE?"

Nothing.

"Hello, Danny?" "Yes, Stockbridge here. You look all weird and shit, dude."

Terry fought to suppress her laughter. Lane *did* look weird.

He was wearing his old toupee, the one he had gotten at first, in his thirties. It had lifted him from the ranks of the almost completely bald and placed him squarely in the midst of all the middle-aged men who appeared to be wearing a hat made out of hair. When perspiration leaked out from under it, as was happening now, the thing seemed not to be in contact with Lane at all, but hovering above his head. The people around the office had different names for it – rat's nest, dirty rug, etc. – but the one she liked best was the one she heard Ellen Cubbage use. She called it "Lane's aura."

No one knew why he wasn't using the expensive one he'd gotten recently, which did look a lot more realistic, but that was beside the point. Lane was sweating under and through his toupee because he was responsible for organizing a company-wide teleconference call. Not that Lane had any handle on the technological side of it. Terry seemed to be the only person in SVI-Jersey City who had taken the tutorial on how to actually operate the teleconference equipment, with its huge, elaborate remote control, and all the steps that needed to be taken, the special operators who needed to connect each participant, etc. No, Terry was setting it up, at Lane's request, and Lane was worried about looking like a fool in front of the Californians. So he was trying to get all the video branches on line first. The fact that Lane had become so desperately dependent upon her made Terry feel a little stronger. And since her review was coming up soon...

Stockbridge, the distribution and sales branch Lane had vacated in a heartbeat as soon as his dream of running Stellar had dropped in his lap, was being run, if it can be said to have been running at all, by Danny Elsmore. Danny was a guitar player who smoked a joint every day at lunchtime with the warehouse guys, from whose ranks he had only recently risen. Although Lane himself had been known to share in Danny's daily indulgence from time to time, and always asked Danny to procure pot for him whenever he needed it, Lane had had a serious heart-to-heart with Danny before leaving Massachusetts.

He lectured him about responsibility, and maturity, and not letting things get screwed up the minute Lane left. The fact was that everyone who knew Danny was worried about his ability to tell anyone he worked with, all of whom loved him, what to do without being laughed at. As things would turn out, that should have been the least of anyone's worries.

Take Lane's anxiety about scrutiny by the corporate guys and his concerns about Danny saying something stupid on the call (or doing something stupid! Would Danny even remember that he was "on TV?"). Combine them with the fact that he didn't know how this stuff worked and he was relying on Terry who, whether or not she did, had every reason to hate Lane's guts, as so many of the low-paid clerical people did. Then add to that the fact that the teleconference equipment, for all its Internet-age wizardry and high-tech impressiveness, at its best delivered a communication system in which there was always a delay of about two seconds between when someone spoke and when the recipients heard the words or saw their lips move. It was enough to confuse even the most well balanced person, and Lane, Terry mused, had not been too well balanced since taking on his new responsibilities.

Becker couldn't believe what he was seeing, couldn't believe what he was participating in. Six tiny but highly efficient speakers were mounted strategically around the conference room. Also mounted on the walls, one at the north end of the conference room, and the other at the south end, were snazzy-looking video cameras. Terry Lunceford was manipulating what looked like the controls of a 747, but turned out to be the remote control for the whole system. And, at the north end of the conference room there was a 50-inch (measured diagonally) high definition monitor. The monitor was showing the people there in the room, and everyone was having fun performing for the cameras, especially once they realized that the cameras somehow had sensors – obviously there had to be microphones – that made them zoom in on whoever was speaking at any give time. There was loud laughter among the fifteen people in the room, and it only increased when the image switched from themselves to Danny Elsmore and the other boneheads up in Massachusetts. They looked like an overpopulated episode of *Wayne's World*! Funniest of all was how Lane was freaking out. Terry must feel sorry for him, George figured, because if she didn't she could be making his life an awful lot worse.

Finally the meeting began. The screen showed four images at once. In each quadrant was a group at a remote location. Going in clockwise order from the upper left, there were Danny and the Juniors (as some of the older Stellarites had taken to calling the Stockbridge team); Cincinnati, with only Fat Mack Foley and two telemarketers in the room; ten frightened kids in Minnesota, looking like they had dressed up for this occasion; and the Davis HQ group. This last consisted of Fallow; Jesse Powell-Portersmith, the sales VP, with his permanent scowl; boy genius marketing whiz Stephen "Sonny" Chess, mild-mannered and weird looking, sporting a ponytail and some sort of decorations hanging at the ends of his long, dangling mustache; Jacques-François Théodore, the 6'3", 185-pound wraith who was their Chief Technology Officer, whatever that meant; and, to Jacques-Francoise's right, little Richie Vinograd, VP of Operations. No one in that room 3000 miles away seemed to see any irony or comedic potential in these two sitting beside one another, Richie's feet dangling an inch from the floor. Killian insisted that the bearded, intensely angry Vinograd only worked as the Circular Operations VP part time, and the rest of the time he played Kramer's midget pal on *Seinfeld*. The resemblance was there. Farthest from the camera were Angela Crofut, the head of human resources; Tondelaya, her assistant, who was controlling the equipment on their end; and Arthur Fishbein himself. Everyone in the room in Davis was looking at the camera or their screen, chatting, waving, laughing, except the owner. Fishbein was pulling olives out of a tall, skinny bottle with his fingers, popping them in his mouth, and licking his fingers.

At last the meeting began. Fallow told a joke and everyone

in California, and Lane in New Jersey, all busted a gut laughing, while no one whose eye George managed to catch even got what the point was. To be fair, the two-second delay would play havoc with the best comedian's timing, and Fallow was no Jerry Seinfeld.

At last they got down to business.

There was one agenda item. Everyone had been asked to come prepared to discuss a new name for the company. One person at each site had collected all the suggestions, and they went around the country reading off the suggested new names.

Fat Mack Foley, looking pleased with himself, read from a clipboard and smiled into the camera after each one. "SCI Entertainment." Grin. "CSI Entertainment." Bigger grin. "Millennium Media. Next Wave Entertainment. ElectricMedia Entertainment.com." Enormous grin. "American Movies and Music Distribution, Inc." Fat Mack put down the clipboard, and two seconds later, his colleagues in four cities saw him do it and realized he was through. Two seconds after that, George and the other Stellarites were astonished to hear a strange sound and see the Circularians nodding their heads enthusiastically and doing something weird with their hands. Oh. They were clapping. Politely.

Several people in Jersey and Massachusetts started to laugh, and Fat Mack Foley beamed. The Minnesota Stellarites were either unable to hear or see anything, or else were too stunned to react. By the time Lane caught on to what was happening and started to applaud, it was too late. The Circularians had already stopped. (Had actually stopped two whole seconds before!) Lane's perspiration began to flow again in earnest.

They continued clockwise from location to location. California went next and they read off a list of about ten names, including Circular/Stellar Media, Stellar/Circular Media, Wombat Entertainment, BiCoastal Media, and Awesome Music and Video. When Jacques-François finished reading them, having rendered them more interesting by means of his Parisian accent, he looked up expectantly. George could hear Dave

Killian singing too softly to be picked up on the mics "Thank Heaven for Little Girls." Danny's crew in Stockbridge applauded enthusiastically, maybe overenthusiastically, which served to embarrass Lane, who, furious at Danny's behavior in front of management, forgot to clap politely, as he had carefully planned to do. Again, he clapped once, too late.

One of the telemarketers in Minneapolis read theirs in a voice so timid that one wondered how she could do her job, which was, after all, talking to people on the phone and convincing them to do something. Her voice was so soft, in fact, that no one could hear any of their titles. Tina called loudly to Terry, "Honey, switch on the closed captioning, willya babe?" She shut up when she realized that the camera above the screen had zoomed in on her as soon as it picked her voice out of the mumbly silence in the room. Tellingly, Minnesota's completely unheard performance received the same polite applause. George and some of the others began to understand. A light was dawning.

Massachusetts had misunderstood the instructions, thinking that they were all supposed to collaborate and decide on one name that represented their branch's best idea. Lane, seething because it would be imprudent to chew Danny out in front of California management, asked through gritted teeth what they had put their heads together and come up with. Danny didn't look at a piece of paper. "Complete Distribution. Or maybe Complete Distribution Incorporated, I guess." Shock. This was clearly the best, least precious, least strained suggestion so far. It was open-ended for the future, it was descriptive, it was simple, it was different and it was strong. Heads could be seen nodding approvingly all over the US. Danny's group applauded themselves and pumped their fists in the air.

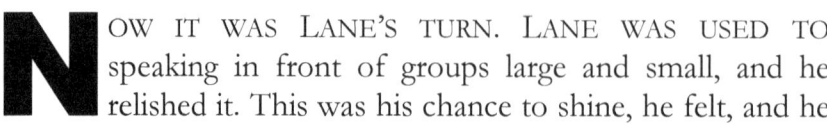

OW IT WAS LANE'S TURN. LANE WAS USED TO speaking in front of groups large and small, and he relished it. This was his chance to shine, he felt, and he was not going to let anyone else read those names. This was key to the future of the One Big Company, after all, and Lane hoped to play a very important part in that. One day people would look back at this teleconference session and remember when they had come up with the name...

He reached around for the clipboard, but it wasn't there. His heart stopped and his head felt like it was on fire, until George leaned across the table and handed it to him. He fairly snatched the clipboard from George, as if George had been attempting to steal a precious opportunity from him. George ignored the gesture and whispered to Lane, "I've crossed off our suggestions that the others have already given."

What a relief. George was trying to help him not look like a fool by repeating something that had already been suggested by one of the others. Good thing, too, because Lane at this moment could not remember a single suggestion that had been made thus far, not even the last one. He was glad George wasn't trying to bury him. He flipped over the top page, and there was their list of nineteen new names – only every one was crossed off but two! He looked imploringly to George, to Kamins, to Lydia, but they were not looking at him.

It's ok, I can handle this, Lane told himself. "I want to thank everyone at every branch who clearly gave this so much quality thought," he began, rising from his chair. "Many of the nineteen suggestions we've come up with have already been mentioned by some of you, which only goes to show that great minds think alike! So—" Lane felt he had extricated himself from an embarrassing situation and made ready to give the names that were left, when he was distracted by a strange, irregular buzzing sound. *What the fuck?* Then he noticed that California's image seemed to be moving toward him, and the people on the edges were sliding out of frame. In fact, their camera was zooming in, though no one had spoken there in minutes. It kept zooming in until one person nearly filled the screen. Arthur Fishbein. With an empty olive bottle in front of him. Snoring as loudly as a contented retiree in his recliner in front of Jay Leno.

Lane was devastated. If a *bon mot* fell in the forest and no one important heard it, had it ever really been said? And could it be repeated at another opportune moment? Sylvia poked Lane, whispering, "Get this fucking show over with, PLEASE?!" Lane forced a smile, and offered "Circular-Stellar Distribution" and "CS Distribution and Entertainment Services." Wait, hadn't people already said these two, too? And had he actually just said two different names, or two variations on the same idea, which probably had already been given? Lane crumpled back into his seat in despair, resigned to his misery.

Fallow concluded the meeting, instructing management at each location to look over their notes – *notes?* Lane realized, in a panic! – and to get back to him with their top three choices. And then each of the cities on the screen winked out. When Lane next looked up he was alone in the conference room. There was a list in front of him in Terry Lunceford's handwriting of all the suggestions that had been made. He gazed at it in confusion for a moment, before he realized what it represented, and when he did realize, he was grateful, though still miserable. He looked up and saw without any reaction the big monitor that was in front of him, on which was an image of him. Taken from the camera at the back of the room, it showed the back of his head, where the toupee had clearly shifted. "What difference does it make?" he asked himself aloud.

THE NEXT MORNING GEORGE DIDN'T GET IN UNTIL almost ten. He'd had a breakfast meeting at the Ultimate with Peachy Importunato, the Warner Brothers rep, in order to see how much money he'd be able to shake out of Warner to get Stellar and its customers through Christmas in high style. It had gone very well, Peachy had found all kinds of funds for them, in return for various favors as usual, some kosher and some maybe not totally *glatt* kosher. In any case, George was feeling fine when he got to the building. He picked up his mail and took the steps to his office on the second floor two at a time. He sat behind his desk and dropped the mail to sort through it, as Groucho Isip came in and sat down, ready to get down to the day's tasks, which were many. The first thing he picked up was a memo. It was from Arthur Fishbein. In it, he thanked everyone for all their hard work on the transition so far, and expressed his pleasure in announcing the new name of the company for which they all worked: Circular Media.

George looked up, disoriented. It had only been eighteen hours since Brian Fallow had said... But now... And no one had even....

Groucho looked at him and smirked. "You didn't know that we all work for 'Circular Media' now? Heck, I knew that last night before I went home!" George shook his head, and forced himself to laugh, and to continue picking up the rest of his mail. But there was something wrong with his stomach, or his throat. One was trying to squeeze its way up into the other, and the flavor of that was on his tongue.

He cleared his throat and then swallowed the last sip of his coffee, which he had taken to go. He tossed the cup in the trash and they got down to work.

The following Monday morning an email from Angela Crofut let everyone know that Circular Media would be reorganizing its management structure for maximum efficiency. The first step was the realignment of titles to more accurately reflect responsibilities and the new, developing reporting structure that was going to be completed, with a new org chart, within the next two weeks. As of that day, every former Stellar Video Vice President was now a Circular Media Director, and the Stellar President was now Vice-President of the video division. Their new Circular Media business cards would be delivered next week. She thanked them for their teamwork and congratulated them on completing the first phase of the integration of Circular Media.

George's phone rang. It was Fat Mack Foley, who never said hello.

"You know what's the most amazing thing about this?" he

began, assuming correctly that George was digesting the same email that he had also received.

"What?" George asked.

"Well, it's – just – amazing. First, she thanks us for doing something that we did not do and were surprised to learn had happened. And then she congratulates us on being demoted."

"Well, I guess that's right. That is exactly what she's doing, isn't it?"

"I'm impressed. She's very good, that one."

PART II
BEGINNINGS

Chapter Eight
Beginning of the End

1997

AFTER THAT, THE CHANGES CAME MORE FREQUENTLY and were more jarring. Ashton Hartock, the accountant, bid everyone farewell a few weeks later. It wasn't clear whether he had jumped, or if he had been pushed, and Ashton wasn't saying. Unlike Dave Olean, who had been his boss back when everything was normal, Ashton did not use his financial experience to move into a high-paying gig in Corporate America. Ashton smiled sheepishly when he told his friends over Ultimate coffee that he was going to work in his son-in-law's gourmet food business. He had often brought pastries and other delicacies to work from his son-in-law's wares.

"What, like I'm going to miss the *fa-kakta* movies I hardly ever watched, with all the *shtupping* and *geschrying*? I'm going to push pencils and manipulate the books and eat myself to death and play with my grandchildren, until I retire which, God willing, will be soon and then I can play with my grandchildren full time."

Indeed, he would not miss the free movies that abounded in the video business as its most ubiquitous and, for some, most coveted perk. But he was going to miss his co-workers, and they him. With the departures of Ernie and Bert, some people had come to think of Ashton as a kind of patriarch, although no one ever voiced this idea. It was clear now, though, now that he wouldn't be around anymore.

"Don't it always seem to go, that you don't know what you got 'til it's gone?"[2] Cubbage quoted Joni Mitchell tunelessly.

That same week, George, Lydia, Lane, Stacy, Hock, Killian, Cubbage and Fat Mack Foley in Cincinnati all received envelopes via Federal Express. The envelopes were filled with information about a three-day meeting they were "invited" to attend in a month, in California. Each of them was to prepare a presentation on the status of his or her department, the current issues, the challenges in the next six months, and their considered opinion on the state of the industry. The immediate effect of these summonses to California, to a formal meeting at a posh resort built in and around a Napa Valley vineyard, was akin to an announcement that aliens had landed and were among us, or that all the managers were going to be stripping down to G-strings for a televised mud-wrestling match. Most of them gathered in Lydia's office, which could barely hold them all, and they all spoke at once.

"What the fuck?"

"So here it is. Here's where they download us, in preparation to getting rid of us!"

"Not necessarily."

"We were warned this was coming."

"But you can't really say that, because they do this every year. All of their department heads have to prepare the same kinds of presentations. They do it every year."

"They do? How do you know?"

"Sonny Chess told me this was coming. He's my new buddy, don'tcha know?"

"Your new boss, don't you mean?"

"Well, probably, but not yet."

"It doesn't matter! If we tell them everything we know, then they have no incentive at all to keep us around. They're not going to keep us out of the goodness of their hearts."

"Well, they have no hearts, so it's unfair of you to expect–"

"I'm serious. We've spoken about this. Do not give them everything you know. You have spent years accumulating the skills and the relationships and the knowledge and the tricks that it takes to be successful in this stupid business. What we have in our heads is worth a lot of money. So don't give it away for free!"

"Whaddya mean free? We all get paid."

"Well unemployment pays $377.50 a week, my friend, and that's what you'll be getting, for twenty-six weeks anyhow, if you hand over the goods. You won't catch me doing it."

Meanwhile, Tina and Kamins and the others who had *not* been summoned had their heads together in Tina's "cubicle," which was bigger than most of the offices in the building. It was positively amazing how everyone seemed to know every significant piece of gossip, both the true stuff and the farfetched fantasies, simultaneously. What were they, an ant colony? Hard to believe there was a collective consciousness or a collective unconscious among people who came to this video island surrounded by razor wire which in turn was surrounded by government-built housing from the fifties, and the enterprising poor who lived there. But no one knew of a better explanation.

As it unfolded, those who were not invited busted the balls of those who were, laughing at their predicament, teasing them about giving a speech in front of the Circular bosses, who would undoubtedly be listening like a panel of judges, measuring each word, each chart, each slide, each byte. *How foolish, to go talk about doing stuff for three days, lose a day going and a day coming back, away from your family for a week, instead of staying here and actually doing what needed to get done! What for, so Arthur Fishbein could fall asleep while they did their thing?! What schmucks to go across the country for that. Good thing they didn't ask me, because I would have said, "No, fuck you very much."*

Yet no amount of teasing could conceal the fact that the teasers envied the teasees, and resented them, and hated the fact that they had not been asked to come and do the very things they were scoffing about. Were they not wanted? Were they not valued? Surely this had to be a sign that they, the left behind, would be the next ones to bite the big one. Kamins, for his part, never let down his guard, but he made a point of taking all the personal stuff from his desk and cubicle, the family pictures and his favorite *tchotchkes* and the picture of himself surrounded by all twelve of the Playmates of the Month for the entire year of 1989, putting them in a big box and sticking it in the trunk of his car to take home. His cube now looked as barren and gray as Dilbert's own.

At the same time, the invitees were also pulled in two different and opposing directions. On one hand were the facts about which they were being busted by their uninvited pals: the unplanned disruption to their home lives; the monkey wrench it threw into everyone's work schedules, not only for the week they would be away, but for all the time and preparation that would go into whatever type of presentation they would each have to come up with. Perhaps most of all was the legitimate fear that they had to choose between A.) look stupid, or B.) hand over on a silver platter their only scrap of job security.

But then, on the other hand, George for one and a few of the others were undoubtedly, well, flattered. George felt stupid for feeling flattered, but it did make him feel a little bit important. Maybe, just maybe, if he made an amazing presentation, and the Circularians could see that he was an expert at what he did... Well, how could they want to let him get away? Bert and Ernie were far from perfect bosses, and they ran their business as little tin despots, and they had some obnoxious qualities, such as Bert using the telemarketing bullpen as his private whorehouse, and Ernie never saying anything to him about it. And they each took away over $10 million, maybe even more, and left without so much as a thank you to everyone who had enabled them to earn it, let alone sharing some of that *gelt* around. Meanwhile, Stellar, or rather The Video Division of Circular Media, or The Company Formerly Known as Stellar Video Inc., was a profit making entity, you might almost say a well-oiled machine. All Fallow and Fishbein and Powell-Portersmith and the rest had to do was leave them alone, and let them bring in the money. Why would they mess with that? Why fix what was decidedly not broken? They may be cold fish, they may be pale, nasty, humorless fascists, but they weren't stupid. They couldn't be stupid.

How could they be?

It was a daunting project, once George got to work on it, and he had to do most of it in the evenings and on weekends, because the day-to-day stuff still had to get done. But it appealed to him in a way. He had never had to do anything exactly like this, not for Bert or Ernie or anybody else he'd ever worked for. He went home that night and taught himself how to use Microsoft PowerPoint.

Frankly, George liked the fact that he was forced to think about his job in this way. And writing about it helped him organize his thoughts in a way that he rarely got to do. One thing he had always complained about during bull sessions about Stellar with B&E was what he had named "management by crisis." Not crisis management, but rather an entire organization that tended to lurch from place to place, in a generally forward direction, but directed mainly by the disaster *du jour*. With rare exceptions, such as the time Olean, Killian and he had pitched the boys on going gung ho into sell-through, most major projects you did at Stellar were in response to an emergency, a complaint, a screw-up, a manpower shortage, a UPS strike, a natural disaster, the sudden loss of a major customer, the sudden addition of a huge new customer who needed everything done differently for no apparent reason, and it all had to be done yesterday. That's when the all-nighters were pulled, the miracles were worked, the astonishingly original ideas were squeezed out, the new short cuts and creative ways of doing things were invented. It shouldn't have been that way.

There was rarely one of these crises (other than the natural disasters, and you would think contingency plans would be in place for those as well) which could not have been averted if someone, or several people, had simply anticipated the consequences of the things they planned to do and let everyone know who needed to know. But it was these crises and the miraculous ways they had managed to do the impossible again and again which had bonded these people together. George only remembered one other place where that had happened. It was 1982, shortly after he had started working for the company, part-time, while he still had his teaching job. It was the crazy early days of the video business, and Bert and Ernie were groundbreaking retailers.

Most of the typical structures and processes that were now followed in today's video stores could be traced back to one store. Their store: Looney Looie's.

Chapter Nine
I Got What You Want!

1970s-
1980s

THERE WAS NO ACTUAL PERSON NAMED LOOIE, OR even Louie or Louis, Looney or otherwise. This was a common misperception among the consumers who flocked into the huge electronics store in the heart of Times Square, and the even bigger "sister" store that was opened in East Brunswick, New Jersey, and among the millions of TV viewers in the tristate area who were constantly inundated with one silly, loud, cheaply-produced Looney Looie commercial after another. They were so bad, so lame, that they had become incredibly popular. Whenever a new one debuted, sometimes during the Johnny Carson show, more often later, because of the cheaper rates, during the Tom Snyder program, it was usually the dominant subject of water-cooler talk the next morning. And people who were otherwise staid, normal, even respectable and intelligent individuals, everyone it seemed took a shot at imitating "Looney Looie," the TV spokesperson, and his signature line, which he always delivered at microphone-wrecking volume: "LOVE ME OR HATE ME, JUST COME

DOWN AND SEE ME– I GOT WHAT YOU WANT! AND I'M TOTALLY LOOOOONEY!!! This last would be delivered while the camera came in closer, closer, sometimes too close to stay in focus, right up until his bulbous, alcoholic's nose looked as if it were going to be crushed by the camera lens at any moment.

And that was when he would do it. Looney Looie – not even the few people who actually knew the actor's name called him or thought of him as anything but Looney Looie – had a strange ability to do something with his face that millions attempted to replicate, but few could come close to matching. It had to do with his facial muscles, and maybe the bone structure of his jaw, and certainly was enhanced by his swollen proboscis and buggy, perpetually bloodshot eyes. When he got to the signature part of his sign off at the end of each commercial, he would lean into the camera and shout "I'M TOTALLY LOONEY!" while shaking his face back and forth. When he did this, he was able to loosen his cheeks, and his lips, and the modest wattle on his neck, and they would *whip* back and forth in a manner so frightening and so violent that his entire face would become a blur, a nightmare image from an insane fever dream. Saliva would fly, his tongue would waggle independently from the rest of his face, his eyebrows would dance independently of one another. It seemed as though all the soft tissue on the outside of his skull was moving back and forth in a wider arc than the skull itself, like the cracking of a bullwhip. The oddball actor had improvised the bizarre signoff, to the initial horror of the commercial's director, Ernie's nephew Stephen Matarowitz. After the first few airings of these commercials, children were said to have had nightmares. Adult viewers thought there was something wrong with their TV sets. Local stations' switchboards lit up.

Today, copies of that first commercial were expensive collector's items. Looney Looie commercials had been spoofed on Saturday Night Live and on every talk show and variety show on television, and in every stand-up act in every cheesy brick-walled comedy club in the country. A specially made Looney Looie ad had been featured in a big Clint Eastwood movie. In the film Dirty Harry walked past a store window where there are a dozen TVs on, all simultaneously showing Looney Looie doing his thing; then it's on a TV at his ex-wife's house; and some of the cops in the police station are seen imitating it, all to Clint's disgust. Finally it comes on during his big confrontation with the bad guy, and Clint whirls and shoots the TV, turns back to the bad guy and, indicating his still smoking magnum, snarls, "Sorry. I can never find the remote." Even better (from the point of view of Messrs. Lehman and Jacobs), such prominent "product placement" in a hit movie could cost a company hundreds of thousands of dollars. In this case, Bert and Ernie had been able to charge Warner Brothers Pictures for the right to associate Dirty Harry with the most iconic, so-bad-it's-great TV commercial in the world. A win-win-win.

Someone from the Academy of Motion Pictures Arts and Sciences had approached them about having their remarkable spokesperson on the 1983 Oscars broadcast. Nobody seemed to understand that LooLoo only existed in commercials; despite appearances to the contrary, he was two-dimensional. He wouldn't even do store openings! Last Christmas season Bert had handed out the grotesque rubber Looney Looie masks that had been all the rage a month earlier for Halloween; of all the things they'd ever been asked to do, this was the one that the employees categorically refused, preferring to be fired than to wear the nasty, airless things.

LOONEY LOOIE'S HAD GROWN OUT OF A SMALL BUT always busy appliance store Bert and Ernie had opened in Brooklyn in the early sixties. They sold "white goods": washing machines, refrigerators, dishwashers. As air conditioning changed from being a luxury to a necessity, they had jumped on that early and they sold more Westinghouse home air conditioning units from their single location in 1963 than Sears did at their top five stores combined. They added TVs and then stereos in 1966, around the time they moved from Brooklyn to West 34th Street and 10th Avenue in Manhattan, where they now occupied the entire first floor, and had offices and stock rooms on three of the floors in the building above the store. That was when they changed the name from B&E Appliances to B&E Electronics, Inc. Always ahead of the curve, they anticipated that plummeting prices and accelerating innovation would begin a crazed demand for "appliances" that were for fun, for lifestyle needs as the marketers were starting to call it.

They were voracious visitors at the very first Consumer Electronics Show held at the Coliseum in New York City in 1967, collecting hundreds of business cards and dozens of samples and spec sheets. Eight tracks, cassette decks, tiny TVs, little speakers with big sound, electronic calculators that could do arithmetic for you in a flash, reel-to-reel tape decks for the home, stereo systems for cars; they drank it all in. That night, over their Glenfiddiches, they saw the future, their future, and it did not include refrigerators and freezers, which took up so much precious floor space. It did include fancy headphones, color TVs with wireless remote controls, 4-speaker quadrophonic sound systems, telephones that looked nothing like telephones had looked for the last fifty years, and little electric staplers that stapled papers without you having to punch them with matching electric pencil sharpeners that you didn't have to crank.

The washing machines and dryers and even the air conditioners were gradually phased out, so room could be made for the fun stuff that was suddenly everywhere in the store, and that was when Looney Looie was born. For several years, Ernie and Bert would take turns going to Japan for big trade shows like Techno Fair, Pacifico Yokohama, Chubu and all the rest. They never failed to come back with new products, which, more often than not, caught the imagination of the New York-area public, hungry for the latest gadget. Though they were still only a "one-store chain" until they opened East Brunswick, which at its grand opening was the largest electronics store in the United States, they had such a reputation among the manufacturers for their canny understanding of the place for new products, their willingness to try new things and new ways of doing business, and their ready cash, (not to mention their abrasive personalities and their legendary sexual appetites while away from home), that Sony made them one of only eight retailers in the United States to have the very first Betamaxes in 1976, which got them tremendous publicity. Once again, in 1979, they were chosen to help Sony launch into America another major, innovative product: the Walkman.

But Bert and Ernie suspected something that even Sony's Akio Morita had not considered. Sony touted the Betamax as a "time machine." It was the heart of their entire marketing strategy. With this incredible invention, you could record a TV program, even if you were watching another one. You could even record a TV program when you weren't home. In this way, you could watch TV shows, sporting events and specials at your convenience. You could play them back whenever you wanted to! In fact, if you liked them, you could keep them. Imagine starting a collection of videotape cassettes of episodes of "All in the Family," or of New York Yankees games? Imagine the lucky housewife who could see both "The Guiding Light" and "General Hospital" despite the fact that they were on opposite each other each afternoon?

That was all nicey nice, Ernie told Bert. But it was a novelty, a fad, and fads, by definition, didn't last. Fads were nice if you prepared to get in before they started, and knew when to get out before you got stuck with a warehouse in New Jersey full of hula-hoops or go-go boots or Official Soupy Sales Shaving Cream Pies ("Ideal for throwing!") that nobody wanted anymore. But Ernie did not think that the Betamax TV recorder, which he had begun referring to as a BTR – ok, his crystal ball wasn't perfect – would go the way of the lava lamp or the pet rock or the Cabbage Patch Kids. Bert was intrigued, especially when Ernie offered to make his point by taking a walk over to one of the porno theaters on 49th Street, between Broadway and Seventh.

They both were occasional patrons of New York's dirty movie houses, like Show-It-All Cinema, the Trylon, and Sexpo America, though they had never gone together before. But this time they weren't going to see a movie. They were going to see a lobby. The lobby of the WonderWorld, which happened to be showing that day a truly remarkable triple feature consisting of *Spiked Heels, The Spy Who Came* and the very popular *Deep Inside Queen Kamarinda.*

They had stopped for hot dogs with mustard and sauerkraut on the way over there, and they were munching these to the disapproval of the seventy-five-year-old, chain-smoking, brassy redhead in the box office with the frightening décolletage which most patrons tried to avoid seeing when purchasing their tickets.

"This better be pretty fuckin' amazing, what you got to show me, if we're paying for tickets and we're not even going in to see the fucking show," remarked Bert, around a mouthful of New York's finest street meat.

"Look, if when we are done you feel you want to stay and see the movie, there is nothing stopping you," said Ernie. "I got places I got to go, people I got to see. And secondly, you didn't pay for your ticket, I did. So fuck you."

Bert laughed his partner off, but muttered, "Still..." as they walked inside together.

The lobby of the WonderWorld, which had once been the old Broadway Movie Palace and which had been around since the time of the silent movies, and only went porno three years ago after having been closed for nearly twenty years, was noticeably free of sleaze, in terms of anything that might get on your skin and cause you to have a disease that would be hard to explain at home. In reality it didn't look much different than it had when Frank Sinatra had signed autographs there in June of

1953, when *From Here To Eternity* was in its first run, with the exception of the fact that the very same glass cases that once framed posters of *Marjorie Morningstar* and *Murder, My Sweet* and *Stop, You're Killing Me!* now held similar-sized posters promoting *The Amazing Adventures of Little Miss Tinkle* and *Heading This Way* and *The Totally Pink Panther*. Autographed 8 x 10 glossies still adorned the walls; but where the images of Harpo Marx and Gary Cooper and Loretta Young and Marilyn Monroe once gazed down in their glittering Hollywood glory, the pictures now all showed naked, large-breasted women with cartoonish expressions, their mouths invariably either shaped like an "O" or puckered for a kiss or with a demure look and a tongue licking the corner of the mouth. These girls all seemed to be pinching their own nipples or sucking one of their fingers, and they had names just as synthetic as their Hollywood forebears: Jade Diamond, Mistress Alicia, Nicki Languor, Sweet Sue Sellers.

Bert did not at first notice what Ernie had brought him to see. That was because there were seven or eight men standing in front of it. It was over on the other side, past the concession stand: a black wire display rack, the kind that holds paperback books or Hallmark Greeting Cards, that you could spin around so you didn't have to walk all the way around it. Only this one didn't hold picture postcards or ladies' magazines. It held little, colorfully packaged, rectangular boxes. Walking over and joining the knot of gentlemen inspecting the items on the rack, Bert selected one and read the name: *Lesbianna Lesbos IS Desire's Sister*. Bert recognized the title as that of a movie he had seen at a theater down the street no more than six months ago, starring Goldy Horn as Lesbianna Lesbos. Was this a book of the movie? It was shrink-wrapped. It didn't feel like a book. The front showed a picture of Goldy Horn, naked, with smaller pictures of other girls' faces in front of each nipple and her crotch. He flipped it over, and found a picture of those same three girls, all servicing Goldy Horn, who had a passably believable look of ecstasy on her face. Bert actually remembered that scene in the film. But what...?

"It's the movie." Ernie knew exactly what was running through Bert's mind; though they were, in many ways, very different types of men, they knew each other pretty well. "It's a movie, a porno movie, on a Betamax tape cassette. You play it in a Betamax."

"The whole movie is on here?"

"Yes."

Bert looked at the shrink-wrapped rectangle in his hand. He hefted it, as if to determine if it were heavy enough to contain an entire, 90-minute movie. He said, again, "The *whole* movie."

Ernie said, again, "Yes."

Bert looked back at the rack. There were more than a dozen different movies, all of the same genre, a most popular one of the patrons of this particular theater and the other theaters like it in the neighborhood. Then he looked at the top of the rack, at the sign he hadn't noticed previously. It said "$59.99!", and nothing else. His eyes half closed for a moment, for no more than a few seconds. He turned back to Bert.

"Six slots high by three, four sides, each slot three copies deep, figure a 100% markup, that's... that's almost seven... that's $6,480 every time the rack turns over."

In spite of himself, Ernest Lehman smiled at Herbert Jacobs. It just so happened that Ernie was afflicted with a smile that always terrified children and discomfited a majority of adults. It seemed almost canine, but his partner Bert never saw anything wrong with it. Perhaps he simply never noticed. "This rack has turned over 100% in the last three days. I checked."

"That's... that's almost sixty grand profit a month! $700K a year," Bert said.

"That starts to run into real money," Ernie said.

"Yes it does," Bert said. "It does indeed. I like that."

"Yes. From one rack. Imagine a hundred racks. Imagine a thousand racks."

Bert was mightily aroused, but, as Ernie had predicted, he was no longer at all interested in watching a skin flick. He looked over at the guys who were snapping up copies of *Lesbos*

Lesbianna IS Desire's Sister, Love Them and Leave Them... Then Love Them Some More, and *Screw or Be Screwed*, forking over sweaty twenties to a girl who looked as though she could not be more than fifteen years old at most, working behind the concession counter. A tall pimply boy with a crew cut was dispensing the popcorn and the Jujubes and the overpriced flat sodas, while the girl-child was taking care of the Betamax sales. She was by far the busier of the two, and Bert quickly calculated that while the boy's average transaction was about five bucks, the girl's was over a hundred. One guy had a stack of fifteen of the Betamax tapes on the concession counter, and was still looking for more. He munched unconsciously from a bag of popcorn as he browsed the rack. Bert's eyes widened and his pulse raced when he noticed that the popcorn-munching guy's stack of Betamax cassettes included two and three copies of some of the titles. *This fucking guy was Christmas shopping!*

Ernie noticed this as well, and he approached the man. "Howya doing?" he asked, trying to tone down his smile. The shopper, disturbed from his concentration on his mission by a man in an expensive suit and a gaudy tie making strange faces at him in the lobby of a porno theater, began to back up. Ernie realized the guy was wary, so he tried to clarify, making it clear that he wasn't a cop or something. "Believe it or not, I'm actually doing market research," Ernie said. "If you don't mind, can I ask you? Are you buying some of these for your friends?"

The fellow didn't realize at first what Ernie was referring to, but then Bert came over and pointed at his stacked up purchase.

"Oh. Oh, yeah, 'smatter of fact I am."

"But do all your friends own Betamaxes?" Bert asked. After all, it was still a very new and very expensive item, and even with Sony's advertising and marketing, the majority of people didn't even know it existed yet.

"No," the man said. "But the way I see it, they will."

Bert staggered. He almost swooned. The air around him was a whirlpool and voices screamed in his ears. Ernie put his hand lightly on Bert's shoulder, and the shorter partner quickly recovered. They shouted "Thank you!" over their shoulders to the man, and moved rapidly toward the door. Suddenly Bert stopped, wheeled, and actually ran back to the rack. He grabbed a copy of *Screw or Be Screwed*, threw a hundred on the counter, and bolted out of the theater, leaving the startled young girl with $37.64 in change in her hand.

ERNIE AND BERT LOST NO TIME. ONCE THEY WERE sure of something, they never wasted a moment. Further calculations were made as they hurried back to the office. Square footage of Looney Looie's that could be turned over to Betamax racks. Dollars revenue per square foot by category. How many pornos came out each year? How many have already come out in the past? Who held the rights to put them on Betamax? There had to be thousands of potential titles. They would have to cordon off the section so that kids and others who might be shocked by the new merchandise couldn't accidentally wander in. Better put a call in to Weitzer the Shyster and have him find out all the ins and outs of the porno business.

They might have to open a separate store.

But wait. There was more.

"Once this thing takes off," Bert pointed out, "there will be hundreds of porno movies coming out on Betamax each year. Guys everywhere will be jerking off at home in front of their TV sets!"

"Go west, young man," Ernie said.

"What?"

"West. California." Bert wasn't following him.

"Bert, take your mind out of your crotch for a second."

"Ha, that's pretty ironic coming from—"

"Movies, Bert. The movie business. Movies."

"'Movies?'"

"Yeah. Movies. You know, Audrey Hepburn, James Bond, Paul Newman, Liz Taylor and Richard Burton..."

"Yes, I know what the movies are."

"Pornos will sell like crazy. I think we see that. But wait until Hollywood gets its fingers into this thing," Ernie said.

Bert looked at his partner in purest admiration.

Chapter Ten
Sirs Laurence Olivier
and Ernest Borgnine

1976-
1978

THE REST WAS HISTORY, THE STUFF OF LEGENDS. THEY took Lane Coutell, a hard-working kid who wanted to go places, and they set him the task of learning everything he could about Betamax and video. One of the first things he learned was that a man named Andre Blay in Michigan had cut a deal to buy the rights to make videos out of fifty of Twentieth Century Fox's best movies, including *The French Connection, M*A*S*H, The Sound of Music, The African Queen,* and *Patton.* Lane would claim famously forever after that he was the person who sold the first video cassette to a consumer, in Looney Looie's. Apparently he meant first non-pornographic video cassette, although he never bothered to include that trifling detail… He had a legend he was building.

Between the crazy commercials and having the lead in offering videos – by this time there were two formats to deal with, Betamax and VHS, a larger cassette – Looney Looie's in

Times Square became a mecca for movie-hungry consumers, especially those with lots of money. Who knew that there was a huge, pent-up desire in so many people, not just in America but around the world, to be an instant movie mogul? One way to accomplish this was to be able to hold "screenings" in your home and invite people over. As video took off, and dozens of new mainstream movies were added to the shelves every month, Bert and Ernie spun off Looney Looie's Video Bonanza, a separate store adjoining the main one on the west side, with just videos, for sale or rental. It was floor to ceiling movies, in beautiful glass cases, and there were TVs mounted high on the walls showing movies at all times, interspersed with plugs by their liver-lipped spokesperson. Looney Looie's had become a New York tourist stop. Among the thousands who paid one hundred bucks each to "join" the Looney Looie rental "club," which got them a club card, a free rental, and the "right" to rent movies for "only" ten bucks a night or buy them for a five percent discount, were Dustin Hoffman, Ringo Starr, Mickey Mantle, Jane Fonda, Robert DeNiro, New Jersey Governor Brendan Byrne, New York Governor Hugh Carey, California Governor Jerry Brown, and many others. One Wednesday night they closed the store early – the video part was normally open from ten am until midnight – so that the Philippines' own Imelda Marcos and her entourage could shop the store unmolested by any actual American citizens other than the clerks. She bought more than 150 movies that night, including everything that featured The Three Stooges, every Walt Disney animated film she and her minions could find, and nineteen "adult" movies (the word "porno" having been banished in the same manner in which certain Italian-American civic organizations had managed to erase the word "Mafia" from the vocabularies of news broadcasters), including one called *The River*, which featured a fetish that many "straights" had not known existed, involving warm water and enemas.

For a while, having Looney Looie's Video Bonanza shut down so that you could be its only customer became a mark of distinction among the uppermost echelon of celebrities and jetsetters, and those who aspired to be thought of in that category. Keith Richards and Mick Jagger did it. Yoko Ono "gave" it to John Lennon for his birthday. The cast of Saturday Night Live held three of their afterparties there during their fourth season. Two Arabian sheiks, one Chairman of Mercedes Benz, Steve Rubell and 40 of his closest friends from Studio 54, a high ranking official of the Russian Communist Party who required utmost security and absolute secrecy, and far too many glittering luminaries who paid ten thousand bucks as well as the price of all the videos they took during their visit. Perhaps the ultimate tributes came when, in the same week, President Gerald R. Ford referred to "Looney Louis" (sic) in a major speech at the New York Stock Exchange, and in the Sunday New York Times crossword puzzle the answer to 76 across, "Video pitchman's complaint," was "IMTOTALLYLOONEY."

By 1979, video stores were springing up all across the United States of America, the price of VCRs had plummeted to less than four hundred dollars, and five thousand different non-adult movies were available for sale or rental to be played in those players, which would soon be in 20% of all of the homes in the country. Despite this daunting inventory challenge, Looney Looie's Video Bonanza established a new slogan for all its advertising: "If they made it, we got it." If a title existed they either had it in stock, or would get it for you, toot sweet. Not a single competitor had the nerve to make the same claim, for the mere reason that it was physically impossible.

Leaving their retail operation, their precious cash cow, temporarily in the hands of the single-minded young Lane Coutell, Bert and Ernie opened B&E Distribution, the forerunner of Stellar Video; now they were wholesaling videos to all of Looney Looie's competitors. They hired a bunch of telephone salespeople, and when there was no more room for them on the floors above the store, or the tens of thousands of video cassettes, now 60% of them VHS and 40% Beta, they crossed the mighty Hudson River and purchased a huge warehouse with offices attached in Jersey City, New Jersey. The building had formerly housed "World Wide Purveyors, Wholesalers of Meat and Meat By-Products Since 1914." While there was no remnant or smell or any trace of the former contents of the building when Bert and Ernie took possession, the local vermin had long memories and could not be convinced that all the meat was gone, and Bert and Ernie had to spend almost $30,000 in extermination expenses in the first year of occupancy.

Shortly after this George Becker, a high school English teacher at the Jersey shore, recalled a discussion he'd had with a colleague over beers and shots in a stinky Asbury Park gin mill. Becker, now a husband and father of a six-month-old boy, sought and obtained a part time job working in the huge, brand new East Brunswick Looney Looie's location.

George's hours at the store soon grew until he was working from 5:30 until ten four nights a week plus a ten-hour shift every weekend, alternating Saturdays and Sundays. With thirty-two hours a week he was considered a full time employee. He worked in the radio department, the car stereo department, the portable stereo department, the camera department, the big-screen TV department, the record department, and finally the video department, which was where he found his home.

George observed that people wandered into the video department, drawn to it, not quite sure what it was that was sold there, but somehow captivated nonetheless. More than a few times he took phone calls from customers who had bought or rented movies and then, when they got home, couldn't figure out where they should stick them into their TVs. He quickly became their best video salesperson and the manager of the video department, largely because he enjoyed talking about movies with the customers, many of whom came back week after week. Some customers' patterns were so predictable that George and everybody in the video section knew that Thursday night was Dr. Lazenback the dentist, about six, and he always rented one or two movies, usually black and white classics, which he would have his wife drop off on Monday morning. Mrs. Coppington from Philadelphia had a standing order to be called each Tuesday at noon to be told what new movies had come in, and she would always have at least one put aside for her to purchase when she came in on Friday. Within a month George came to know some of the rental customers so well that sometimes he would put a couple of videos in a bag and put their name on it. When they came in he approached them with the bag, pressed it into their hands as if it contained the plans for D-Day, and told them to leave without browsing the shelves. "If you don't absolutely love both these movies, I'll pay for the rental myself. Trust me."

And they did trust him, because he was usually right. George hadn't thought of himself as a "movie buff" prior to getting involved with video and Looney Looie's, but he realized that he'd become one inadvertently. New York area television viewers got to see lots of movies on TV in the fifties and sixties. He'd watched the Early Show most evenings since he was eight-years-old, and the Late Show almost nightly since he was twelve. He'd been a fan of The Million Dollar Movie which would show the same movie four times a week right around the time he got home from school. Sometimes he watched it more than once in the same week, which was why, without trying, he realized that he knew all the dialogue of *Mighty Joe Young*. Later, as a teenager, he'd hit the Regency once a weekend to see whatever was new; all of this had gradually given him an almost encyclopedic knowledge of movies, and his naturally sticky memory and love of arcane details had made him a movie trivia champion. He began spending his prep periods at his day job at Monmouth Regional High School writing movie recommendations, trivia quizzes and reviews, all to be used in the store to pique the interest of customers.

It was these, which he posted around the department and handed out to customers and salespeople alike, that really led to the big change for George. He was neatening a pile of new ones on the counter on a Saturday morning in spring when Heidi, his assistant manager, made a "warning face" and indicated with a look someone who had just entered the building.

George followed her gaze and looked and saw Lane Coutell. He didn't think Coutell was one of the owners of Looney Looie's, but he was rumored to be related to them.

Although this big shot from the city was visiting, surveying the store, its employees and customers like a farmer overseeing his chickens, George was too busy to care. He'd gotten involved with a couple of regular customers.

James Franklin had just snared the last copy of George's newest movie trivia quiz. George assured Mr. Ainsworth, escorted by his two impatient little girls, that he'd sent Heidi into the back room to make more copies. While he waited, James, an intense young black man with a small goatee and wire-rimmed glasses, quizzed the older white dad from the sheet in his hand.

"'Who won more Oscars for acting, Sir Laurence Olivier or Ernest Borgnine?'" James asked him.

Ainsworth laughed in surprise. "Come on, that's ridiculous! It's got to be Olivier. How could it be McHale from *McHale's Navy*?"

"It's your worst fear come true," replied the younger man. "It's a tie! Olivier won for *Hamlet* in '49, but Ernie B. took one home for *Marty* in '55."

"*Marty*. I'd forgotten all about *Marty*. And *Olivier* only won for *Hamlet*?"

"According to this, Sir Larry got himself nominated eleven times, but, other than a couple of honorary awards, which we both know don't mean jack, he struck out all but once."

They both looked over at George who shrugged. "Don't blame me!"

The older guy's girls were tugging at him impatiently. They probably knew that their father could spend an entire Saturday in this place, and they had things to do. "*Marty*," he repeated, ignoring their pleas to leave. "That was a good movie. I bet I haven't seen it in twenty years."

His new friend offered the signature *Marty* lines: "'What do you wanna do tonight, Marty?' 'I dunno, what do *you* wanna do tonight?'"

"Hey, you think they have that movie here?"

"They well might, man. They sure got a lot of movies. If it's out, if it's on video, supposedly they got it here."

George offered to search out a copy; when he got back, Mr. Ainsley's girls had won the tug of war, so he told Franklin that their only copy of *Marty* was out, rented, and he'd be glad to reserve it for him when it came back in a day or two. James was amenable. To remind himself to follow up George removed a piece of string about 8 inches long from his pants pocket. The string was blue. He tied a little knot in the center but before he could stuff it back down into his pocket, the other part of his brain recognized that the phone had been ringing for a long time, so he answered it.

When he hung up he noticed something that concerned him a little. It was Lane Coutell near the cash registers at the front of the store, talking first to Mr. Ainsley, and then to James Franklin. He was too busy to think about it, though. The department was crowded. But a minute later Heidi poked him with her elbow. He looked where she was looking to see that Coutell was headed their way.

Now what? It had been a rough week. Whit, the baby, had had them up three nights in a row, and George had spilled coffee on his grade book, obscuring half the grades for the marking period, with report cards due in only a couple of days. The last thing he needed was any aggravation from management at his not-so-part-time job.

"You can buy batteries anywhere," Lane began enigmatically, even before he got to George's counter. George's boss's boss was speaking to him, but he could not for the life of him figure out if this required a response from him. Lane must have realized that he wasn't making sense, because he explained, "I just saw a man – no, two men – who came in here, on a Saturday, when they really didn't need to buy anything."

"How do you know that?" asked George.

"I know that because the one guy walked out without anything, he was in a hurry. And the other guy bought a magazine and batteries, something he could have bought in his neighborhood, at a corner store, anywhere."

Completely clueless as to where this was going, and starting to wonder if Lane Coutell might not be just a little bit nuts, George asked, "Well, why do you suppose they came in then?"

It was a logical question. The store was in the parking lot of a huge mall, but it was separate from the mall. There were three acres of cars between Looney Looie's and the huge indoor shopping center. You had to *want* to go there to go there. You didn't walk by and get drawn in because you saw a TV set in the window.

"Apparently, they came in because of you."

"Me?! What– Why– Why, why would they come in to see me? None of my friends came in so far today."

Seeing a blue thread on the counter, Lane absent-mindedly picked it up and made to toss it into a nearby trash receptacle. George politely but purposefully snatched the thread from him. "Sorry," George mumbled. "I need that."

Now it was Lane's turn to look at George like maybe *he* was crazy. George steered the conversation back onto whatever kind of track it had been on a moment earlier.

"You were saying that people came in to see me? Why would that be?"

Lane shook off the little distraction. "You make up those sheets, those sheets..." He looked around, took one off the counter behind him. "These, for example. *What's New in Movies for You?*" He found another sheet. "*Movie trivia for the week of May 12th.*' You do these every week, right?"

"Well, yeah, I guess. Usually, as long as I have time. I've just been doing it for the last few weeks. Is there anything– "

"'–wrong with it?'" Lane finished his sentence for him. "No, I would say not, there's nothing wrong with it. But in the fifteen minutes since I've arrived here today, I saw two customers who came in here because they knew that these would be here today.

"And they wanted them."

Now it dawned on George: He was being *complimented*, not criticized. It was a huge relief. Then the relief gave way to something else that he couldn't quite describe, but he knew it felt good. That afternoon, the feeling had dissipated to a great degree, but whenever George recalled the exchange with Lane, and in particular the look of happy amazement on his face, it came back. He tried to define the feeling during his drive home, and when he pulled into his driveway, he had pretty much pinpointed it.

It was the warm glow from a gratified ego.

GEORGE GOT A LOT OF SATISFACTION FROM HIS teaching job, but never from his boss, Elizabeth Creighfield, whose sole purpose in life was to point out the shortcomings and failures of the teachers in her English Department, especially those of the younger male teachers. Weekly plans turned in late, failure to follow the curriculum precisely enough, being a little too happy in your work – these were some of the things that really ticked off the Crayfish. All the strokes George ever got that made him feel like what he was doing was worthwhile and that he wasn't a total loser came from his students. Frankly, it had never occurred to him that there was any other order of things. Bosses were to be tolerated, avoided, circumvented. Possibly learned from, maybe even emulated in some cases. The satisfaction had to come from the work. It made sense.

But today he had felt really good because someone whom he had thought didn't even notice him or his contribution to the business – hell, he never thought that he *made* or *could* make or *should* make a contribution to the business – this person, who was, by all accounts, the right hand man of the actual owners of Looney Looie's, had gone out of his way to praise what he had done and thank him for doing it.

George couldn't feel any better if he had planned the whole

thing. But it never would have occurred to him to plan a thing like that.

Everything was different after that. Alice May was waiting by the door with a scared look on her face when he got in. She had taken a message from a growly sounding man named Bert Jacobs an hour ago. He'd left a phone number with a 212 area code that he wanted George to call.

Three nights later, George drove into the city to have dinner with Lane Coutell and Bert Jacobs at a fancy restaurant on Lexington Avenue. Actually Bert complained the whole time about the food and the service, but it sure seemed fancy to George. Alice May and he didn't eat out much with a baby at home and a teacher's salary and his part-time income from the store, and when they did, the fanciest they could afford was a better-than-average diner by the beach in Avon. Things were not likely to get any easier for a while, until Alice May's maternity leave from her teaching job at Rutgers was over and she went back to bringing in a paycheck again.

Lane and Bert were really nice to him. They kept asking him about his family, and about teaching. They asked him what he thought of the store, and if Ralph Bongiovanni, the store's manager, was a hard-working guy. George was shocked to be asked by the owner of the company to pass judgment on his own boss. But Lane and especially Bert could not get enough of George's opinions, and eventually he warmed to it. Finally they got around to asking him about the stuff he wrote and brought into the store.

"Well, the fact is, talking to people who come in about movies is, well, it's fun. I probably shouldn't tell you that, because if it's fun how can it be work, right?" Nervous when he sat down, George had drunk a cocktail a little too quickly before dinner and now he was into his second glass of red wine. "But it is, it's fun. Those sheets I make up, I just do that when I'm between classes and I don't have anything I've gotta do. It's like doing a crossword puzzle. Only different."

"Kid, what I'm gettin' at is, why do you think the customers like that stuff so much?" asked Bert, who had begun to look to George like an oddly well-dressed leprechaun.

"Well. See, people who come in there, into the department, they like movies. But sometimes they just don't know what they want. It's easier to figure out what you want to get if you have a list of what's just come in lately, as opposed to the stuff that's been there. Because there's so many movies. Too many to see everything. Don't get me wrong; that's a good thing. It's like, it's like, what's the expression? An embarrassment of riches. Yeah. It's a little overwhelming for the customers, especially the new ones, and we get new customers all the time."

"Your membership has doubled in the last six months." Lane said.

"I know," George said. "We sell new memberships every day now."

Bert poured more merlot into George's glass, then wiggled it above his head to let the waiter know they needed more.

"Makes sense," Lane said. "They say 20% of the homes in the country will have VCRs by the end of next year."

"'Embarrassment of riches,'" Bert said, rolling the phrase around in his mouth and in his head. "I like that."

"Right," George said. "So anyhow, to keep everything fresh, we keep reorganizing the videos. Every couple of months. That way the store – I mean, the department looks different and it's more fun for people who just like to browse."

"How different?" Bert said.

"Well, after the new year, we put all the movies in alphabetical order, A to Z, regardless of what they were. In March we changed it, we made one section for comedies, one for action flicks, one for mysteries, and like that."

"By genre," Lane put in. Bert shot him a deadly look to make sure he wouldn't interrupt again.

"This month we changed it again, and grouped everything according to what studio it's from. It's not boring."

"I tell you what would really help though, now that I think about it."

Bert was listening. "What's that George? What would help?"

George had never heard a more pronounced New York accent, outside of a movie or a TV program, but he stopped himself from saying that out loud. "What would help would be if there was one place, like the card catalog at the library, where you could look up what movies we had, and what other movies we could get if you really, really wanted them."

Where was this coming from? he wondered. He hadn't planned on giving a frigging speech at this dinner. He hadn't planned on opening his mouth except to eat. He wasn't used to having adults listen to him, only teenagers. This was different. "Of course, a card catalog would be bulky, it would take up too much room. What would be really good, I think, would be a book with all the movies in it."

"A master item list, we have that," Lane said.

"No, yeah, no, we have that, yeah, but that won't do the customer any good, and we can't show it to them anyhow, because it has wholesale prices in it, right? No, what would be really good, what I would like if I were a customer, would be a book with all the movies in it, but the book would have everything that a card catalog at the library has. Let's say you wanted to see, say, a Humphrey Bogart movie, but you don't remember which one. You could go to one place and find a list of all the movies he was in. But let's say, on the other hand, you weren't necessarily a big Bogey fan, but you wanted to see a real film noir detective flick: you could look up *The Maltese Falcon*. Or say you saw *The Adventures of Robin Hood*, with Errol Flynn, and you really liked the style, and you wanted to see what other movies were directed by the same person, but you don't remember the director's name. You go to *Robin Hood*, it tells you it was directed by Michael Curtiz. So you go to a page that lists all the movies he directed, and *boom!* There's *Casablanca*!

"And when you got to the page with the movie on it, it wouldn't just be the name. It would have a description of the movie, like a little paragraph, and who's in it, and when it came out, and who directed it, and all that stuff."

"A directory," Lane said.

"A catalog," Bert said.

"And they could take it home with them. *That* would be cool," George said, finishing his wine.

"But there's thousands of fuckin' movies already!" Bert said.

"And more coming out every week," Lane said.

"Yeah," George said. "It would be hard. But it would be a good thing. I've never seen one. But I can picture it in my head perfectly."

Chapter Eleven
The End of the Beginning

1979

AND SO IT CAME TO PASS, THAT SUMMER, THAT George took the train into the city each day. They put him on the fifth floor of the building away from all the other offices. To do what they proposed to do, without tools that would not be available for almost ten more years, he needed a lot of manpower: people to type, people to look stuff up, people to organize things. Lane brought in a printer who was a friend of his and had him talk to George, and they made a plan. George would give the printer, a small, sincere guy named Stuart Kranz, whose plant was in Secaucus, New Jersey, as many typed index cards each week, on Friday, as he could. Each one had on it all the relevant information about a movie. Wednesday the following week, the printer would send over nicely printed, long, narrow, glossy sheets with the stuff that they had typed all neatly done up in real print, like a newspaper or a book. Lane found them a guy he called a paste-up guy. The paste-up guy was a middle-aged, dangerous-looking, suspicious-smelling fellow named Bellicranz. He didn't seem to have any other name, just Bellicranz. Bellicranz would take the strips of nicely printed movie summaries – synopses, the correct plural of synopsis, George insisted on calling them – and slice them up and glue them into place. He also figured out how to take pictures of the video boxes, and pictures of the 8 x 10 black and white glossies of movie star glamor shots and scenes from old Hollywood treasures, all so they could be used as illustrations for the new catalog. George had found literally thousands of the old black and white photos in an old file cabinet, and prevailed upon Bert and Ernie to let him hold onto them "just in case they might prove useful." Every week, Bellicranz would make pages of their book. Their catalog. George was impressed with Bellicranz's skill as the pages began to look like a "real book," and Bellicranz made each one look interesting, different from one another and yet clearly all part of the same unified and ever expanding whole. It nevertheless creeped him out every time he watched the twitchy guy wielding an X-acto knife.

Each week it got harder, and it also got hotter as the summer broke records. There was a grand total of one room-sized air conditioner, on a floor that looked like an abandoned factory, with dingy windows, peeling paint, weird convoluted pipes that seemed to go nowhere useful, ramps, steps, and assorted junk on grey metal shelves and all over the floor, all in a space the size of Monmouth Regional High School's gymnasium.

But as it got harder, Lane kept sending him more people. George explained that as things got more complicated, more sets of hands and eyes would be the key, and Bert, who visited their floor only occasionally, was of a mind to let Lane provide George with whatever he needed to get the job done. By the 4th of July, there were, in addition to Bellicranz and George, Anthony Fiorentino, a chain-smoking bantamweight Mafioso wannabe who couldn't hurt a fly, Andrea Sasso, a girl of about twenty from Queens who invariably wore at least one and sometimes more skin-tight articles of clothing with a leopard-skin print who could type about 500 words a minute and Ellen

Cubbage, an NYU grad student who, when she wasn't sorting index cards or typing descriptions of movies, taught two sections of undergraduate English composition as well as a class called "World Without Men."

And that wasn't all. There were five young interns from Borough of Manhattan Community College, Sheri, Shari, Shirley, Shauna and Bob, all of whom were very fond of marijuana, and would smoke it up on the roof of the building any time they got a break. There was Jean Jonas, who could write synopses better and faster than George could, and who didn't have to be told that *synopses* was the correct plural of *synopsis*, and Dolores Coutell, Lane's cousin from Coney Island, a shy, chubby high school dropout. Maybe their most unique hire was Dr. Esperanza Isip, a genius at organizing everything who, before she had emigrated from the Philippines to avoid being murdered by a deranged ex-husband, had been a licensed periodontist with a thriving practice. Apparently the American Dental Association didn't accept Philippine certification. Esperanza would have had to take two years of additional courses, despite all of her successful practical experience. That would have cost more than she could afford. In addition to her practice, her home and her family, she had left behind all her money.

Their huge space was filling up quickly, not only with people but also with equipment and furniture. They had acquired three artist's drafting tables and at least a dozen desks and folding tables, no two alike. Bellicranz had asked for and Lane had found them a machine to put glue on the strips that Bellicranz cut just by passing them through it, like a wringer on an old fashioned washing machine; Bellicranz referred to it as a waxer but everyone else called The Stickifier. As long as big purchases were being approved, Bellicranz suggested a gigantic contraption called a stat camera; the unfortunately nicknamed printer Stu the Jew had loaned them one. Bellicranz trained almost everybody how to use these devices. The stat camera enabled them to take pictures of anything to create illustrations. They got a used Xerox copier and a car stereo with a cassette tape deck and two gigantic speakers in boxes covered with dirty yellow shag carpet which had come out of the back of a van that Fiorentino had sold "to some mook who forgot to ask if the stereo came with it." A tall bookshelf loomed behind George's desk, with forty different reference books about the history of movies and TV. They had four industrial strength fans on tall stanchions without which they would not be able to breathe. And along one wall were stacked cartons and cartons of index cards, pens, pencils, paper, X-acto knife blades, glue, wax, tape, photographic supplies, copier ink and other assorted necessities.

As July approached August, the "boards," which were actually white, 12" x 15" shiny cardboard sheets that the pages were positioned on after Bellicranz finished with them and George gave them a final check, were stacking up pretty high, and Esperanza's green boxes of file cards had grown from one to sixteen, each neatly labeled with the name of a movie genre, and with little blue dividers separating sections in each box alphabetically. Everyone had a job, writing, filing, researching, cutting, pasting, statting, copying, proofreading, re-proofreading.

On a Thursday night at the beginning of August, at about eight o'clock in the evening, George found himself sitting at a round table in the back room of a Mexican restaurant on Ninth Avenue. The official name of the place was Taco Joe's, but everyone called it I Got Yer Taco Right Here, because why wouldn't they? Also at the table were Dolores, who had actually begun to speak audibly, Esperanza, Stu the Jew, Jean, and a guy who had started working with them just that morning, the impossibly named Hakizimana Wasef, a dark-skinned kid from some country in Africa. Possibly Egypt. They were sharing a series of cold pitchers of Rolling Rock, rubbing the backs of their necks and the lids of their eyes, and bitching and moaning amiably.

Stu seemed pretty content, and he kept the waiter hustling for more pitchers and more nachos and guacamole. "It looks like you're pretty near finished, right?" he said to George.

"'Finished?'" Dolores repeated. Apparently it had not occurred to her that all this was anything other than an ongoing process. George glanced at her briefly, surprised that one of the people who had worked with him most of the summer did not see the bigger picture, just the daily grind. He couldn't imagine doing all the work without a clear vision of the result, but now that he thought about it, it was possible that Dolores wasn't the only one.

"Well, you're right that we're almost finished with the main part of the catalog." Everyone looked at George, who took a sip of his beer. "But I'm not sure how long it will take to do the index. The indexes."

"Indices," Jean corrected him.

"Right," George said.

"You're gonna index all the movie titles and the page numbers they appear on," Stu said. "That's a good idea."

"Well yeah, that," George said. "But we also have to do an index of all the actors and actresses, and what movies they're in." Stu the Jew made a cranky face.

"And what about all the porn?" Dolores spoke up. Jean sprayed her mouthful of beer and everybody laughed. But Dolores was not wrong.

"It's true, we gotta do a listing of all of those. Can't forget the porn."

"Synopses?" Esperanza asked, beginning another round of rowdy laughter and lewd jokes, in which several people gave their versions of how a synopsis of a movie whose major plot device was the arrival of a TV repairman at a house shared by three ridiculously large-breasted clothing-phobic co-eds might read. Jean, Dolores, George, even Hakizi-whatever-it-was took a turn, getting more and more descriptive with each try. They were really getting silly. It was five pitchers into the evening, which by George's math was five-sixths of a pitcher apiece. But since Stu, he had just noticed, was nursing the same glass of vodka he'd ordered an hour before, it really was a pitcher apiece for the rest of them. On average.

"Lemme ask you this, George," Stu said. "About how many movies will be in the book, all told? Fuggedabout the pornos for the moment."

George did calculations in his head, noticing that math was easier for him when he was a little drunk. "Not counting *All About Eva* or *Tied, Trained and Transformed* or any of those, I'd say somewhere north of six thousand."

"And each movie, each synopsis mentions how many actors?"

Jean spoke up. "Most list just one or two stars. But some have three, four, a few have more."

"Can't put in Groucho and Chico and leave out Harpo," George said, spawning a Marx Brothers imitation contest at the table, which Esperanza won when she killed everyone by doing Groucho's low slung walk around the table. She didn't smoke so she grabbed someone's lit cigarette out of the ashtray, waggled her eyebrows menacingly, and, in her Filipino accent kept repeating, "That's the most ridiculous thing I ever hoid!" Jean laughed so hard she eventually started coughing and choking and waving her hands. Dolores Heimliched her even though she had nothing stuck in her throat, which did more harm than good. Then Stu got up and got her a glass of water, which she sipped when she had calmed down enough. Tears covered her face. "Oh my God," was all she could say, quietly, when she was able to speak, and almost began to laugh again.

"That's fifteen thousand, maybe more, actors." Stu was persisting in his line of inquiry.

"Right," George said.

"Don't forget directors, there's one of those for each movie," Jean put in, even now still breathing erratically, teetering on the edge of self control.

"Right," George repeated. "We gotta index them, too."

"Six thousand directors," Stu said.

"Not nearly," Jean said, holding a hand alongside her face so she couldn't see Esperanza, because now the very sight of her threatened to send Jean back into hysterics.

"But you said..."

George explained. "Don't forget, most directors in the book directed more than one movie."

"Oh, of course, right. But still..."

"John Huston directed half of 'em," Jean offered. Then, "Only a slight exaggeration."

"And most of the actors played roles in many different movies," George said. "Christopher Lee has at least fifty roles,"

"Seventy," Esperanza said.

"So there's not nearly fifteen thousand actors," George said.

Another pitcher of beer arrived, greeted by groans and cheers. Everyone seemed to be having a good time except Stu, and everyone besides Stu was having too good a time to notice that Stu was not. But when George nearly poured Rolling Rock into Stu's glass of vodka, Stu jerked his glass back, and a little beer sloshed onto the plastic tablecloth. George looked at Stu and realized he wasn't participating in the merriment, despite the fact that he was paying for all of it.

"What?" George asked.

"Hm?" Stu took a moment before looking up from the spot on the table on which he seemed to be concentrating.

The jukebox may have been playing the whole time they were in I Got Yer Taco Right Here, but George only noticed it for the first time as a new song by an unknown band came on.

> *You get a shiver in the dark*
> *It's been raining in the park but meantime*
> *South of the river you stop and you hold everything...*[3]

"Stu. Hey, Stu, what's on your mind, why so quiet, hm?"

"Well, see. You're new to this, right George?" Stu continued as George nodded in enthusiastic agreement. "I mean, you're a teacher, right?"

"Yup. Last I checked. That is, they renewed my contract."

"So, you're going back to school, what, day or two after Labor Day?"

"Something like that."

Stu sighed. For the first time in the admittedly brief experience of anyone at the table, the printer sounded a little put out. One might even have detected a hint of miff. An aroma of sarcasm. "Well, have you asked yourself, 'Self, when will this job be done? When will we send it to Stu to print?'"

"Well, pretty soon, I guess..." George sounded lame even to George. "I mean, the main part is done."

Resigned now to the unpleasant task before him, Stu took a breath. "Please, don't take this the wrong way, George," he began, "but you have got to pull your head out of your own ass and take a look around."

The table went silent. This was completely uncharacteristic of the accommodating, almost wheedling printer. Since they'd met him, the only thing he seemed to know about ass was how to kiss one. Before George or anyone else could struggle to formulate a reply or a question, Stu said what he had to say. "It was my understanding that I was going to have finished boards by the first week of August or, at the latest, the 10th. I guess I got that information from Lane, and now it appears that you and he have never had such a conversation, I can see that clearly now. So let me ask you this: when does this catalog need to be put into the hands of customers?"

George was suddenly stone sober. He realized in that moment that the work he had been doing all summer was fun, an extension of what he already liked to do. It was fun working in a business, instead of a school. It was fun having more money than usual to spend, even getting a babysitter and taking Alice May out to a movie and a late dinner. But he realized now that there must be some strings attached, that it couldn't all be fun. For the very first time in his life but not the last, the muscles in his upper back, across his collarbone, and in his neck began to tighten. The skin around his skull prickled in a most unpleasant way. He actually had to alter his posture in the chair awkwardly in order to make peace with the way in which his autonomic nervous system was reacting to the approach of an unknown negative stimulus. George started to answer Stu, tried to say something about the autumn, but he stuttered.

Stu plowed onward. "Because, I need to tell you this. If I don't have all the boards, every last one, in the plant, no later than–" he paused while he consulted a worn pocket calendar book filled with paper clips, Post-It notes, and scribbling in every square – "no later than August 27th, the last Monday in August, here is what is going to happen. My presses, specifically the press I need to do this job on, the one *you* need me to do this job on, *that* press will not be available after that date, until–" he flipped a page in his calendar and traced it with his finger. He flipped another one. And another one. "The press will not be available again until the Monday after Thanksgiving."

There were several intakes of breath around the table. Not from George though, because he wasn't breathing. "But then..."

"But then it's too late," Stu finished for him.

"Yeah but..."

"I'm sorry. You guys are great, but these are physical realities that I can't change. Even the 14th is pushing it. Understand: Lane asked me if I could do this book, and I told him when the press was available. Then Bert beat me up on price. I mean, we're gonna do this job for half of what we would normally charge. Why? How can we afford to do that? You've heard the expression 'Time is money?' Well let me tell you boys and girls, press time is big money. I was able to give Bert and Lane the crazy price they wanted, because they promised to fit this job in to one of the very few open periods we had on this press. There are jobs I can juggle around *before* the 14th – if you were ready to go now, for example, I'd bump the job that's on the schedule for this week, it wouldn't matter, they wouldn't even notice, because we're *ahead* of schedule on that one. But if you're a day late getting it to me – I'm saying that this is what we call the drop dead date, no flexibility – if you give me this job on the 15th of August, you won't get your books before December. Maybe January."

Jean spoke up. "But, by then, all the data–"

"–will be out of date." Stu was getting remarkably accurate at finishing their sentences. "Because this whole thing is all about what's the newest? What's the latest? What's hot? Right?"

Five heads nodded meekly.

"And we'd miss the Christmas season," George said. "People really like to buy videos for Christmas presents."

"Of course they do," said Stu. Now everyone was watching the discussion between the two men like a tennis match between an old pro and a popular amateur.

"But Christmas... Christmas is so, so... I mean, Christmas is so many months from now!"

"In one sense, that's true," Stu said. "But in another sense, Christmas is now. Now."

"Now, if you could do this without all the indexes–" He looked at Joan and corrected himself. "Indices. If you leave out the indices, then you're done right now. Right? Right, George?"

Now everyone was looking at George, including the waiter who stood there with a seventh and as it would turn out superfluous pitcher of Rolling Rock. "Just about. Pretty much. Only... See..."

Then, "It's no good without the cross reference index, and that's no good without the title index, and it would be ridiculous to put it out without the listing of triple-X," Joan declared.

"And laser discs," Dolores reminded them. She had just begun working on compiling all the movies in that new format.

"See," he said again, and then, without conscious forethought, George did something that he rarely did. He told a lie. "I promised Ernie and Bert." What he really meant was that he'd promised them he'd make the catalog that he, George, had envisioned. *Was it technically a lie?*

George looked up at Stu in the vain hope that the printer would offer him the solution. Nobody wanted a book that wasn't going to be useful. They had worked too hard, even if they had been too stupid to realize that they needed a schedule for completion. George was miserable, and miserable in a way that he had never known before. It gave him a nasty, metallic taste in his mouth.

Stu didn't offer a solution. Instead, he offered one more problem.

"And have you thought about exactly how you're going do these fucking indices? Have you ever created an index before? If you had one of these computer databases, that would be one thing. But you have to do it by hand. You may not be able to do it without months of work. Do you know, could you tell me now, step by step, how to make this index with all the actors and directors?"

George felt as though, had Stu asked him if he, George, could tell him the date of his, George's, birthday, that he wouldn't be able to do that. What on earth had he been thinking? He started to feel his perceptions begin to distort. Titles of movies, names of actors floated chaotically in his field of vision in no recognizable pattern. Stu looked very far away, and all the sounds in I Got Yer Taco Right Here were muffled, as if coming through a wall. One sound pierced through the ambient noise: it sounded like the pealing of a bell, but it was actually an electric guitar. And then a strange, dispassionate voice.

He can play the honky tonk just like anything
Saving it up for Friday night.[3]

Across the table, Esperanza drained the last of her beer mug, and gently placed it back on its coaster. Trying but failing to suppress a colossal burp, she said, in her own voice, "I know how to do it."

ESPERANZA'S SOLUTION WAS PRETTY INVOLVED, BUT when George and the others thought about it, it seemed like it ought to work – in theory at least. She had been doing nothing but filing and organizing on the catalog project, and she had done a lot of filing and organizing at her last few jobs, and she had worked in her periodontal practice without an assistant for a good part of the time, meaning she had had to take meticulous care of records and materials. Her idea was that they would use the original index cards they had made. Of course she had saved them, even rescued them from the trash when someone who thought they were no longer important had tossed them out. The only thing was, they needed, she figured, at least twenty people.

Each person would get about 300 cards to start with, one movie per card. It didn't matter what cards everybody got because this list would have to be alphabetized by the actors' and directors' last names, but they'd be given out in alphabetical order anyway, just in case, for unforeseen reasons, that wound up mattering later. One person would be the typist. One person would run around making sure everything was going smoothly. She described it the next day, at work, and Ellen Cubbage said, "Like a great big bingo game."

"More like gin rummy," said Esperanza. "You win when the cards in your hand are used up."

So that was the plan. George now realized that if they were going to get the boards to Stu's plant by the 14th, that Monday, then he would have to work the calendar backward, like he should have done months ago. Index was easier for Bellicranz to paste up than the pages in the "guts" of the book, because it was all straight lists. It would take him no more than a day. They'd only put in pictures if they needed to fill an empty space. Stu's people would need about four days – ok, better figure a week – to get the type set and get it back to George. They also needed to do the "regular" title index. Esperanza wrote out a plan for that, as well as lists of the laser discs, and the even newer discs from RCA called CEDs, and the pornos. Cubbage insisted that it was essential that they separate the gay porn from the straight porn. It was more of a political stance for her than a marketing choice, but it probably made some sense anyway.

By the time everybody went home on Friday night, the third of August, everything else in the book was done. In fact, it was out of their hands and at Ballistic Web Offset in Secaucus.

But they couldn't start, Stu had explained, until they had every single page. Stu explained the technical reason, but it frankly didn't matter to George and his team.

By George's calculations – and he had Cubbage and Joan and Stu check him, and they agreed – they had to be done by Friday, the 24th of August. They could do it. They would all take off the weekend, and then, on Monday the 20th, they would start working, and they wouldn't stop until they were done.

They could do it.

It would work. It had to. They shook on it.

Shauna flipped on the big office stereo, to an FM station. And there it was, that song again, the one that seemed to be everywhere that summer.

> *We are the Sultans,*
> *We are the Sultans of Swing.*[3]

GEORGE ARRIVED AT WORK ABOUT 7AM ON MONDAY. He hadn't been able to sleep much all weekend anyway, so it was more a matter of relief than deprivation to rise so early. Alice May got up with him at five and made him breakfast while he threw some clothes and his shaving kit in a duffle bag. When he kissed Alice May goodbye, they both felt as though they were in a movie scene in which the young bride bravely holds back her tears as her new husband heads off to an uncertain future, to fight a war in a distant land. Although Alice May was still a little pissed that George might be gone for the whole week, she'd accepted the idea that it had been unavoidable. Or that it would've been avoidable, if George had had any experience whatsoever in doing this sort of thing, or if the people he worked for had not neglected to give him and his crew a few requisite pieces of information. Alice May increased the intensity of her Tuscaloosa, Alabama accent. (She normally kept it at a barely perceptible 2; now she dialed it all the way up to 10 – the dreaded Scarlet O'Hara setting.) She hugged George goodbye outside on the driveway. She kissed him and bent her left leg at the knee and she said, "I'll wait for you, George. As long as it takes. And I'll write every day!" Rendered like this, *George* sounded like it had two distinct syllables, and *write* sounded like the name of a rodent. She fluttered her eyes and held George's face in her hands.

"Yeah, well, that won't be necessary. I'll call you each night, and you can call me whenever you need anything." George wasn't playing the scene, but Alice May continued it, because the show must go on.

"You look so brave and so handsome in your uniform!" she did declare, getting that breathy thing going in her voice that made it sound more like a northern actress affecting a Dixie accent, not the way any southern girl she knew had ever spoken.

George smiled at her performance, although in reality he was feeling pretty crappy about the week to come, and just a little bit scared. If Groucho's plan – Esperanza had left the Mexican joint with a new nickname that would follow her the rest of her life – didn't work, it was George that everybody would be mad at, not her.

He saluted Alice May and got into the car, put on his seat belt and started it up. There was a red and yellow plastic bubble-blowing pipe on the passenger's seat. He picked it up, clenched his teeth around it, rolled down the window and, changing the setting of the scene only a little, said "I shall return." It was quarter to six; it was already 80 degrees, and it was always hotter in the city.

He wasn't sure if anyone else would come literally prepared to work around the clock, since in retrospect he thought that he had not made that clear, but to his amazement most of them did. And many people brought people. Andrea brought her girlfriend Lizzy who dressed exactly the same as she did but leaned more toward the zebra prints than the leopard. The five stoned kids from BMCC brought along three more stoned kids. Dolores brought Estelle, her mom, Lane's aunt, about whom she assured George, confidentially, "Don't worry, she's cool."

George couldn't even imagine what Dolores meant by "cool" in this particular situation, but one thing was certain, this was definitely not the Dolores who had arrived there in June. Lane was there, mainly because George had called Bert over the weekend to explain the situation, and why they might be running around the clock on their floor for a few days so they might need a few supplies. Bert figured out what had happened, and had called Lane and chewed him out about it and told him to pitch in.

Joan brought her little brother, Stephen, who was fourteen. George was a little concerned about a kid who reminded him of his students being there, especially for all-nighters and all that stuff. Joan acted surprised. "What? He can read, he can hear, so he can play rummy," said Joan. "And don't worry, he has seen and heard everything before, so we don't have to be on our best behavior around him."

"Hey," said the kid.

"Hey," said George. *This is getting weird*, he thought.

Cubbage, Anthony, Groucho (who obligingly waggled her eyebrows every time someone called her by her new name), Lane and Joan gathered around George's desk, and they finalized their plan of action. Cubbage would grab a helper and work on all the "other" stuff – the regular title index, and the separate listings. Andrea, of course, would type, and the remaining seventeen of them would play rummy. Cubbage commandeered Hock, the new guy; together they loaded onto a rolling cart a Xerox copy of the guts of the catalog and a bunch of reference books, and wheeled it over to the far end of the floor, where they set up a typewriter and some dividers so they wouldn't interfere with the main event and it wouldn't interfere with them. Groucho gathered everybody into the open space in the middle, Lane and Dolores moved the table with the typewriter over there, and soon they all had a stack of 4x6 index cards in their hands. George would be the floater and the caller, and he also held a smallish batch of cards. Everybody else had almost 400 cards.

Shirley was selected to be in charge of the stereo, which had become both a necessary and a controversial part of their environment, never more so than it would be this week. All factions agreed upon Shirley, and she promised to satisfy everybody's musical preferences in turn. On the table where the tape deck sat there were three to-go boxes from the Carnegie Deli, and all three were filled with tape cassettes of music. Shirley announced that they would start with disco, and then switch to something else when the tape ended. Even Joan, who sometimes wore a "Death to Disco" T-shirt to work, agreed that this was a good plan, and that disco might get this extraordinary experimental endeavor well launched.

Shirley popped one in, turned it up and hit play.

> *Ahhhhh, Freak out!! Le Freak, c'est Chic,*
> *Freak out…*[4]

"Everybody ready? You got the rules of the game? OK, let's start."

So George began by asking everyone if they had any actors whose last names started with Ab- . Bob immediately hollered in protest.

"What about Aa- ?!"

"You got an Aa- ?" George thought the kid might be too stoned to work. "Who? Someone named Aardvark?"

"My man, Willie Aames," he replied proudly, spelling the curly haired young actor's name. "Star of one of my personal favorites, *Zapped*."

George acknowledged that he was right, and that with people's last names, he shouldn't assume that any particular combination of letters was out of the question. "Especially with Polack actors," Anthony pointed out helpfully, as Bob stood up and did a brief, celebratory "I-got-the-first-one-and-George-was-wrong" dance. Andrea's girlfriend Lizzie hit Anthony in the back of the head with one of her cards. "Hey, how was I supposed to know you was a Polack? Nobody knows your last name." So this was how it was going to go, George worried.

"Kind of ironic that the actor who starts with Aa- starred in a movie that starts with Z- ," commented Shari.

"That's not irony," corrected Shirley. "That's coincidence."

"Look," said Joan. "If we have this much discussion about each and every actor or letter or whatever, we'll be lucky to finish before New Year's, and I think my boyfriend is expecting to see me before then, so I think we're going to have to set a pace and keep moving."

George was grateful that Joan had said it, so things like that didn't always have to come from him. "Any other Aa-'s?" he asked. Thankfully there were none, and they moved on to Ab-'s.

Under Ab- there were Abbott & Costello whom they agreed to lump together, and Walter Abel, a guy who had been in a 1947 movie about a talking dog called *The Fabulous Joe*. Sheri began to espouse a belief in the possibility of speech in dogs, but several people shushed her. They weren't on a roll yet, but they were trying to get on one. As each new actor was named, Andrea started a card for him and put it in a box. George would come by periodically and rearrange them so they were consistently in alphabetical order.

By the time they had gotten to Am- – surprisingly Don Ameche was the only one – the crew was starting to grumble. "Listen," said one of the new BMCC kids, "You gotta go a little slower. We have to look through all these cards and pick out actors' and directors' names, and some of them have more than a couple. Can we at least cross them out after we're done with them?"

Good question. George looked over at Groucho, who had protected these cards from destruction and in so doing saved his ass. Were they now going to destroy them? Once the cross-reference index and the alpha index were done, they would just be redundant. He could tell Groucho knew what he was thinking and was against it. Stephen, the middle school kid, made a smart suggestion. "What about those note-taking pens? You know, the yellow ones?"

"Highlighters!" screamed out Sheri and Shari. If they

highlighted each actor on each card as his name was used, it would be easier to scan through them. They'd be looking among fewer and fewer unhighlighted names. And when all the names on a card were highlighted, that card could be – not thrown away, marked with a small X, and put back into a big box for later re-alphabetization.

This made sense. There was an office supply store they always used just two blocks away. George looked at the big clock in the shape of a flying boat on top of a giant's head. It was a promotional item from Paramount Pictures for *Time Bandits*, which was still in theaters but would be out on video before Christmas. He saw that it had taken them almost four hours to get only to Don Ameche. He didn't want to do the math about how long it would take to finish at that rate. Joan read his mind and reassured him. "It's gonna go faster and faster as it goes on. First of all, it gets easier each time we cross out an actor's name. And it gets easier each time we ditch a whole card. Plus, we'll get better at it as we go. We'll get there." *Maybe she's right. I'll know*, he figured, *by the end of the day tomorrow.*

He declared a fifteen-minute break during which people should "pee fast, and smoke 'em if you got 'em." Since the graphics supply place wouldn't deliver for a sale of only fifteen dollars, George gave Joan a twenty to go to the store for the highlighters, and he called the Carnegie Deli to deliver lunch. Their number was scrawled on the wall above the telephone. He started to give an order but before he could he was told that their order was already on its way. Mr. Jacobs had called and arranged for regular deliveries of three meals a day for 25 people. By the time Joan was back with the highlighters, everyone was eating pastrami sandwiches, slurping split pea soup from enormous paper bowls, and enjoying other oversized delicacies.

George asked Cubbage how their part was going. "It's boring," she said, "but it's moving along. We take turns reading to each other while the other one types. That kid can type almost as fast as me. We're up to the F's. We should be able to finish the title index by sometime tonight. Someone other than us will have to proof it. Then the CED list, the laser disc list, the 'how to use this book' page, a key to all the different abbreviations, the Table of Contents, and then it's just the smut and we're done. Then we'll come and help you guys."

"Do you want to switch off? Let somebody else do what you're doing and take their jobs?"

"No," she said adamantly. "I started this, I know where everything is and how to do it, I'm more familiar with the titles than almost anybody, I better finish it."

"Okay, okay."

Andrea caught George's eye and tapped her watch. "All right everybody," he called out. "Take five more minutes to finish up. We're starting again in five minutes."

By eight that evening they finished all the B's. Two letters down, twenty-four to go. It did not look promising. But Joan had been right, they kept getting a little faster at it, fewer hiccups and stops and wait-a-minutes. Maybe if their pace kept accelerating...

They had by that time finished disco, heard two Beatles albums (to the chagrin of the college kids, but not, surprisingly, of Stephen), a bluegrass tape, Devo, the Tubes, Vivaldi's Four Seasons, Frankie Valli's Four Seasons, Twisted Sister, and a collection of old blues legends. They had also managed to eat their dinner – the Carnegie had sent over hot entrees and cold drinks – without shutting down the rummy game. Some ate while others continued, then they switched, and after a while they were all eating and working. Bert had come up and visited during the afternoon. He consulted with George, wanted to know what else they might need. George made a couple of suggestions, and Bert thanked everybody for working so hard, and he left. He hadn't spoken to Lane directly, and, although Lane tried to act like it didn't bother him, several of them noticed that it obviously had. Shortly after Bert left, his secretary came upstairs with a huge coffee urn and several pounds of Maxwell House.

By ten they were up to Elisha Cook, Jr. (*The Black Bird, Born to Kill, The Maltese Falcon, Rosemary's Baby* (!), *Shane, Stranger on the Third Floor, Tom Horn*). D was in sight, and George was slightly more hopeful. Four of the eight college kids had left a little past eight, but that was not so bad, because Lane had gone down to the store and offered the clerks overtime if they came up after their shift. Six of them did, and though they had to learn the rules of the game as beginners, their familiarity with the movies soon made them better at it than almost everyone else.

They heard the freight elevator come up to their floor, and two delivery men had George sign for a dozen army cots and a bunch of blankets and pillows, too. George called Bert at home to thank him for all the support and all the stuff.

"Sorry there's only twelve cots, kid," said the gravel voice. "That's all I could scare up."

"Don't worry, that's great."

"All you kids are very friendly. You'll just have to sleep together," he suggested.

"That might not be the greatest idea," said George. "But we'll probably be taking turns taking naps anyway, so this will be great."

There weren't many more than a core group of about a dozen rummy players who could stay overnight anyway. At midnight, when they had just finished Kirk Douglas (seventeen movies, *Champion* through *War Wagon*), Joan made Stephen take one of the cots over to the far side of the floor. The rest of the group pushed on until almost 2am (Fellini, Federico: *Amarcord, Clowns, 8 ½, La Dolce Vita – La Strada* was not available on video yet), when Joan, Anthony, Andrea, Dolores' mom, and a couple of others had to lie down. The rest took a short break and vowed to push on.

George went to check on Cubbage and Hock, whom he hadn't seen or thought about since dinner. From behind their divider came the clack-clacketing of typing. Peeking around, George saw that Cubbage was typing and Hock was sleeping. They had found a ratty old easy chair, and he was out cold in it.

He was wearing gym shorts and a sleeveless Allied Moving T-shirt. His feet were resting on Cubbage's leg, and one of his flip-flops had flopped onto the floor. He was drooling just a little. Cubbage shushed George.

"He just fell out," she said, "in the middle of a sentence. It was actually cute." Cubbage did not normally do cuteness. "I figured I'd let him rest. I can do this part just a little slower without someone reading to me."

"I'll give you one of my people," said George.

"No, don't. I'll wake him up in an hour. It's getting done. We're ahead of schedule."

"Well then why don't you sleep some too?"

Cubbage said, "I don't sleep." George knew that it wasn't worth one's time to argue with a short declarative Cubbage sentence, so he left them and went back to rummy.

When dawn broke over Tuesday George awoke and was appalled to realize that he wasn't home with Alice May, about whom he had been dreaming, but rather was on an army surplus cot on the fifth floor of a west side building in Manhattan, and the light which woke him was filtered through windows smeared with dirt and grease that dated from World War I. The rummy session had ground to a halt when they'd finished the three Fondas who had more than forty movies among them. As his whereabouts solidified around him, George took solace in the smell of fresh coffee, the sounds of two typewriters, and several people calling out movie titles and actors' names. It now had a life of its own, this thing.

Andrea and Lizzie returned at nine. They had explained that there was no way they were spending the night and working tomorrow without a shower in between. When George pointed out that there was a shower downstairs between Ernie's and Bert's office that they had permission to use, Andrea looked askance at Lizzie and told George with a shudder of revulsion, "If you think I'm getting naked, anywhere in this building, especially in that little freak's shower—" Lizzie made a finger-in-the-throat "gag me" gesture – "you have got to be nuts."

Andrea had had a run in with Bert, who tended to be a caveman around sexy women. George said, "Fine, I was just offering. I understand."

Tuesday went pretty much as Monday had. Indeed, they continued to get better at it as they did it, up to a point. The fact that they had eliminated almost a quarter of the cards made things easier, too. It never quite cooled off on the fifth floor. The huge industrial fans on their tall stanchions had to be pointed on an angle toward the ceiling. A few windows were kept open for circulation, but the reality was that they didn't want the air outside to come in, because it was hotter and more humid than the stuff they were breathing.

Around mid-day George was headed to the men's room, but took a detour over to Cubbage and Hock's corner. He could hear Hock reading titles to Cubbage, who was typing them. "*Angela, Fireworks Woman. Any Time Any Place. Anyone But My Husband. Around the World with Johnny Wadd. Audra's Erotic Ordeal.*" George heard Hock snicker at the last title, and Cubbage did too, but there was something else in her voice. They continued, "*Autobiography of a Flea. Babbette's Needy Mouth.*" George thought he heard Cubbage take a sudden intake of breath. He left without poking his head inside. On the way back from the bathroom, unable to help himself, he went and eavesdropped again. They had come to the infamous *Bodacious Ta-Tas.* Cubbage was reading to Hock now. "*Bodacious Ta-Tas: Bambi Learns a Lesson. Bodacious Ta-Tas: Bambi Busts Loose. Bodacious Ta-Tas: Barbie's Nipples. Bodacious...*" There was something theatrical in Cubbage's reading, it seemed. George couldn't imagine her saying "*Hell in the Pacific. Hello, Dolly! Henry V*" in quite the same voice. Something interesting was going on.

They had a disaster at seven-thirty, as some of them were finishing dinner. There were heavy duty cables all over the floor just begging to be tripped over. Dolores' mom hooked her foot on one and crashed into one of the fans, knocking it over. The thing made a hell of a racket as the cage surrounding the blades broke, and the blades continued to spin, shooting off sparks as they scraped against the hard floor. Estelle wasn't hurt, but before anybody knew what was happening the fan rolled over on its side and blew thousands of index cards into the air. It also banged against and knocked over the typewriter table, and spilled all the new cards too. Everyone stood there with their mouths open for what seemed like forever, and then Estelle started to cry. Dolores and Cubbage and Joan and George all tried to comfort her, assuring her that it would not be that big a setback. Then everyone ran all over collecting the cards. They had really flown far, some of them, and George realized that it was possible that not many, but a few of them might have flown out an open window. He thought about running downstairs to the sidewalk, but he dismissed the idea as ridiculous. What next, would he inch out on a ledge above 34th Street just to snag a ten-word synopsis of *Nyuk! Nyuk! Nyuk! Best of the Three Stooges Volume 21*? In that moment, George came to grips with the fact that the cross-reference index was going to be… imperfect. In fact, in all likelihood there were a couple dozen mistakes here and there in the catalog. He didn't say anything to anyone else, but he made himself be okay with that. *As long as it doesn't get out of hand*, he told himself.

The group realized, too, that it didn't matter if the cards were in any order or not. They just needed to be divided up and they needed to keep going, and in very little time, they were doing that. Luckily the typewriter that fell, a 35-pound Underwood, was built like a battleship and had suffered no significant damage, and the cards Andrea had typed were all in one pile on the floor, because those did need to be in order. Everyone got back to work. Shauna put on a Bob Marley tape and it started with "No Woman, No Cry." "I didn't even realize!" she said.

"Coincidence, not irony," Sheri cut her off, before she could say it. Dolores ruffled her mom's hair, and they began to get back into their groove with a smooth reggae beat.

N THE OTHER CORNER, HOCK AND CUBBAGE WERE nearly finished with the long list of pornographic, or "adult" titles. Hock was reading, Cubbage typing. *"Susie Sucks Sally. Swan Dive. Swagger. Swashunbuckling. Sweat, Steam and Sensuality."* Cubbage stopped him and asked him to give her that last one again. *"Sweat, Steam and—"*

"Say it slower."

Hock did. He went on. *"Sweet Angela's Education."*

"Yes," said Cubbage. She was typing slower now too.

"Sweet Dreams of Your Love."

"Slower. OK, go ahead." Cubbage's NYU T-shirt was rolled up, and she was rubbing her belly.

"Sweet Syrup."

She wasn't even typing at all anymore. "Mm."

"Sweet Taste of Honey."

"Yes. Yes."

"Taste Me."

That was it, Ellen Cubbage had reached her limit. She tore off her shirt and pounced on Hock. She hooked a toe into the waistband of Hock's gym shorts, and in a second he was completely and impressively naked. They kissed passionately, riotously, voraciously. They slipped onto the floor and Hock rolled on top of her, stripping off what clothing of hers remained. In a second he was inside her, and she made a gasping sound. She froze the action for about a second, and she looked up, listening for anyone who might be coming by, if anyone heard.

"Fuck me, now, I don't care who hears."

And fuck they did, right there on the floor, like a couple of people who had spent eight hours in foreplay without touching one another. In retrospect, it was amazing under the circumstances that they had gotten as far as the T's.

THERE WERE NO DISASTERS ALL DAY WEDNESDAY. *Woo-hoo.* By the time they broke for dinner, they were at Pickens, Slim (*Blazing Saddles, Dr. Strangelove*, and half a dozen others where he didn't spoof himself, but after those first two, who cares?). The only problem was that just as they were getting good at it, people started dropping out. Joan had to run home to take care of her mother, but she left Stephen. The store people all had to go do their regular jobs. Estelle, Dolores' mom, left for a made up reason. She had already given her all, both before and after the fan incident. Lane went home on Tuesday night to get a change of clothes, but he didn't come back. Anthony left "sick." Andrea left when she lost a contact lens, but promised to be back as soon as she could get another one. Amazingly, her best friend stayed. They were down to only three of the college kids, George, Cubbage, Stephen, Dolores, Hock, Groucho, and Andrea's friend Lizzie. Fortunately, Hock and Cubbage were finished with everything else. Once they finished Z in the cross-reference index, it would be over.

When Shirley left she'd deputized Shauna, who stuck with it, to be in charge of the music. Shauna, to the surprise of George and the disgust of Joan, slipped in a cassette containing the soundtrack from *Saturday Night Fever*. Groans and cheers greeted the Bee-Gees' falsetto:

> *Whether you're a brother or whether you're a mother*
> *You're stayin' alive, stayin' alive*[5]

Stephen jumped into the middle of the room and began a terrible imitation of John Travolta's dance moves.

> *Feel the city breakin' and—*[5]

The music stopped.

The lights flickered, then went out.

The fans coasted to a stop, and so did Stephen. The first thing that went through George's mind was that the silence was such a relief. The second thing was that the power was out.

"Don't panic!" he shouted into the darkness.

"We're not panicking!!" the others shouted back in unison.

George felt his way across the floor, tripping over boxes,

tables, chairs, articles of clothing, a cot, a desk, another cot, and a carton of 3 pound cans of Yuban, before he finally found the wall that led him to the door into the stairwell. The light out there was blinding after fumbling through the dark, but it was the emergency power light. That meant that the whole building was out. From the window in the stairwell on the 5th floor George could see that a section several blocks square, but not the entire island of Manhattan, was dark. He could hear people on floors below him, and he could see customers pouring out into the street from Looney Looie's, lit only by the passing lights of cars. George sat down on the top stair and leaned against the wall. It didn't matter if there was an earthquake or a nuclear attack or a plague, if they didn't finish by Friday, they were screwed. Should they all troop across town to a hotel? Who had money, or even enough line of credit on their credit cards (the few who had them) to pay for enough hotel rooms for nine people (although it was becoming clear that there were some who would not object to bed-sharing).

"Whaddya think, Becker?" Cubbage sat down on the landing next to him and handed him a beer. "We have to drink these up before they get warm. That's the rule during power failures, and you have to do your part."

"I think I'm tired," George said. "I want to see my wife and my kid. I want to never see an index card again, or hear the sound of a typewriter again. I want to be finished."

"We will be pretty soon. Don't flake out on me now."

"I was going to suggest we all knock off early today and go home for the night and get back at eight tomorrow morning. Now... ?"

"That would have been a terrible idea. We would have lost the rest of the potheads, and maybe others. Groucho's got a horrible cold, which means by the time we're done we'll all have it. We can bring it home to our loved ones."

"What difference does it make now? This could be it. The power might not come on for a day or two. We're essentially fucked."

"Only if the power stays off. Usually they fix it right away. Whatever happens George, you did a pretty good job. Yeah, you didn't plan well in the beginning, but none of the rest of us thought to ask you when we had to be finished by, and it's not because we're afraid to ask you questions or make suggestions. If we don't get it to Stu in time, we'll take the boards back and take it to another printer. Printers call all the time looking to make us a deal."

George looked at her. This was what passed for effusive praise and emotion from the normally nondemonstrative Ellen Cubbage. In fact, something about her looked a little different, George noticed. Probably it was the halogen lights in the stairwell.

"Thanks Ellen."

She made a face to play off the near-tenderness of the moment. "But I still think we'll finish."

"I just wish the power would come back on. We would finish as fast as we could, no breaks, and go home and stay in bed for a week. I gotta start teaching in a couple of weeks."

And just like that the lights and the sound and the fans came back on. Cheering could be heard from the street.

—everybody shakin'
And we're stayin alive, stayin alive.
Ah, ha, ha, ha, stayin alive.[5]

"Becker, that was pretty impressive. Now say, 'I just wish Ellen Cubbage had four million dollars.'"

He said it. It didn't happen. They went back to work. On Thursday afternoon, at about three, when only Cubbage, Hock, Lizzie and Groucho were there working, George said the magic words, the ones they had been dying to hear: "Has anybody got any Z's?"

Of course, everybody had Z's. All they had left in their hands were movies like *Pajama Tops* starring Pia Zadora, *Romeo and Juliet* directed by Franco Zeffirelli, and *Who Killed Doc Robin?*

starring George Zucco. It was four o'clock. They were done a day early.

"No Adolph Zukor?" George asked. He couldn't believe it was finished.

"Go home, George," said Groucho. "We are finished."

"Zukor made hundreds of movies."

"Maybe they weren't that good," suggested Hock. "I mean, if they're not on video." George could not remember ever hearing his voice before, other than when he was reading porno titles to Cubbage. "But who names their kid 'Adolph'?"

"In a previous century, probably lots of people in Hungary and Austria did."

"Oh."

It was quiet for a moment. A wisecrack-free moment.

Then, George said, "Okay, then we're done."

They high-fived, packed up, and left. They discussed FedExing the last of the material to Stu the Jew, but George wanted to drop it off in Secaucus on the way home. Stu had given Bellicranz a little space and an art table at the printing plant. Ballistic would crank out the type over the weekend, Bellicranz would paste it up on Monday morning, and George would stop in later that day, around noon, and give the index pages a quick eyeball. Monday, August 13th. Drop dead day.

George had been told by Ernie and Bert not to worry about the cover of the catalog, so funnily enough, this thing he and his team had worked so hard on… they had no idea what it was going to look like on the outside. They had their hands full getting pages 1 through page 398 exactly how they wanted them.

A week later, on the Monday before Labor Day, George poured himself a cup of coffee in his kitchen. He had taken a week off before going back to work in the store, and this was day he was going back. Next week he'd go back to his classroom and his students. He was about to take his first sip when he noticed that Alice May who was reading at the table over her coffee, as she always did, was humming strangely. *What is she reading that has her so rapt?* he wondered. Alice May stopped humming, began singing: "La, lalala la la, dum-de-dum…"

It looked like a magazine, but a really thick one. Craning his neck, he got a glimpse of the cover. Oh. It was a color picture of Looney Looie making one of his goofiest faces ever.

Alice May looked at George expectantly. There was a brief moment of disorientation, and then George literally felt his eyes widen, his eyeballs absolutely bulge.

"Is that…?"

"It sure is!" She yelled it so loud that Will, dozing in his highchair, woke up to see what the hell was going on. He wasn't impressed. He played with a little lump of oatmeal, rubbing it into his forehead.

"Gimme!" George said. "Lemme see it!"

She yanked it back, away from his grasping hand. "This one is mine," she said. He thought she had gone insane, until she reached to the center of the breakfast table and removed a dishtowel that had been hiding a stack of three more catalogs. *How had he not noticed* that *before?* "That one, the top one is yours! The Fed Ex guy came early this morning. I'm sorry I didn't wait to let you open it. I just couldn't."

"It's fine," he said as he removed the top book from the stack. Alice May had customized one special copy for him by taping a quipu on the cover, an eight-inch piece of red string with a knot in the center and two shorter blue strings tied on to the left side. The quipus made Looney Looie look like he was not only loony, but also very exotic.

Looie had, with the help of creative photo montage work, two videos in his left hand – *Kramer vs. Kramer* and *Star Trek The Motion Picture* – and three – *Electric Horseman, Love at First Bite,* and *Meatballs* – in his right. His eyes were so loosely arranged in his head that he seemed to be looking at the videos in both his hands as well as at the viewer all at the same time.

George sat down at the kitchen table. He was stunned. He couldn't open it yet. He looked at his wife, who was watching him with an uncontainable smile. Then she jumped onto his lap, hugging and kissing him, and telling him how proud she was. "You don't have to leave for the store for almost half an hour. Look through it!"

First he flipped it over, finding Kermit the Frog, Miss Piggy, Fozzy Bear, Gonzo, and the entire lineup of Dr. Teeth and The Electric Mayhem, doing their zany best to pitch the video of *The Muppet Movie* on the back cover.

He turned it back over and opened it. The inside front cover had a color ad for TDK blank tape. Facing the TDK ad was their title page. It looked a little bit like a movie poster for a movie called *Looney Looie's Video Catalog*.

Beneath the title, almost looking like movie credits on a poster, it said

Conceived, written, designed, and assembled by

and then it listed all the main players' names in alphabetical order, then gave a tip of the hat to the Borough of Manhattan Community College internship program. Beneath that was the copyright date.

He flipped through the first few pages. How could something be so familiar-looking – after all, he had proofed them and studied them and reorganized everything down to the tiny 8-point font copyright line at the bottom of the title page, with the year in Roman numerals – and yet so utterly different? It was baffling. It was delightful. It was three-dimensional.

"Wow," he said.

"Wow, indeed," Alice May said. "And you did it. First you imagined it and now… look, see, *voilà* … here it is."

Now he began to riffle through the pages, stopping every few seconds to examine a page more closely. It was like a little miracle. *She's right*, he thought. *This is what I pictured and now it's real.*

A dark cloud passed over his face. "What if there are mistakes? What if I see a mistake?" He closed it, as if afraid to accidentally see a typo.

She pinched him. Pretty hard. "*If* there are any mistakes, you'll probably be the only one who notices them."

"Ow."

"But if there are *no* mistakes, *none*, then we have a different problem. Because that would mean that you are not human, which would make that thing over there—" she directed his attention to Will who was now working oatmeal and strained peaches into his lank, silky blond hair, purposefully, as if it were the first item on his day's agenda "—is a half-alien, half human baby."

Y ES, THE CATALOGS CAME OUT, AND LOONEY LOOIE'S had the best fourth quarter in its history by far. Bert and Ernie asked what George thought they should do for the people who worked so hard. He suggested bonuses, and that's what they did. Bert had somebody in payroll mail George a list of everybody's names and start dates. George put one, two or three stars next to each name, based on his assessment of their level of contribution. From this information Bert or Ernie would determine the amount each would get.

On top of their hourly wage and the massive amount of overtime they earned at time-and-a-half by working four days straight, in the first week of October they got bonuses. The college kids and Stephen got $300 bucks each. Lizzie, Hock, and Estelle got $600. George insisted that Groucho, Cubbage, Joan, Andrea and Dolores get the most. They got $1000 apiece. He never found out how much Lane was bonused for the catalog. He understood that that was between Lane and B&E, and he was glad not to be in the position to have to make that call.

George got $3000. He spent some of it on a party for everyone who had worked on the catalog, on the night before Halloween, at I Got Yer Taco Right Here. He spent some of it on plaques with peoples' names on them and a picture of the catalog's title page, with the words "I MADE THE WORLD'S FIRST VIDEO CATALOG," and T-Shirts bearing the same slogan. And he spent the rest on a long, romantic four-day weekend with Alice May on Martha's Vineyard, during the time he had off for the New Jersey Teachers' Convention.

George was back working at the store, but had cut back his hours a little. He needed to concentrate on his work at the school. He was tenured, he had been there seven years, he knew what to do and when to do it. It didn't pay much, but there was the satisfaction.

During her maternity leave, even with George gone as much as he was, Alice May had managed to do a ton of research. She was expanding her doctoral dissertation on tribal conflicts in the Peruvian Andes into a major work. When her maternity leave ended they were able to hire Angela Kersey, Ward Kersey's granddaughter, as a nanny, because MacMillan Publishing had given her a contract for the book and a $2500 advance. Two months later she was promoted to Associate Professor of Archeology in the Anthropology Department at Rutgers. And next year she would be leading a small expedition to Peru for a couple of weeks. It was entirely funded by the National Geographic Society, and Rutgers was giving her a yearlong sabbatical with full pay enabling her to do the travel and the research, and to put it all together as a new book.

On a Sunday in November, George got a call at the store from Ernie Lehman, asking him to come work for them full time, in the office, not in the store. He would do marketing stuff, advertising stuff. "You're a creative kid and you're a hard worker. This thing is only going up and up. Be a part of it. You just might like it."

Ernie wanted to know what George's salary would be for teaching that year. George, who would one day learn the ABCs of negotiation and become moderately effective at it, answered him truthfully: $17,241.80. Ernie offered George $35,000 if he would start in two weeks. That was more than he made working both jobs now. For about four seconds, George thought about it. George said January. Ernie said ok. George said, "Then I guess we have a deal. Thank you."

Ernie said, "Thank you, Mr. Director of Marketing."

"'Director,'" George repeated the title. "Who am I directing?"

"You'll figure that out after you get here."

They hung up. When he got home that night he looked up marketing in the dictionary. Over the course of the following year George would hire Groucho, Joan, Cubbage and Hock to work full time.

On Monday, he gave notice to Mrs. Creighfield, the English Department head. On the day before Christmas break, he said goodbye to his students. Somehow he had not anticipated what an emotional conflagration that would bring about. But it was done.

And that was that.

PART III
ENDINGS

Chapter Twelve
The Go-Ahead

1997

THE ANNUAL PLANNING CONFERENCE IN CALIFORNIA
went just about as well as the Stellarites had expected.
The setting took them by surprise, however.

It took place in a posh resort nestled among the rolling hills
and lavender vineyards of the Napa Valley. The purity of the air
and the flavor of it were so delicious that they briefly forgot to
maintain their apprehension about the three days to come.

George, it turned out, arrived a few hours later than the
others.

They'd all been booked on a Newark-to-San Francisco
direct flight. They had a nine-seater rental van waiting in which
they would drive the ninety miles to Napa, no doubt singing "99
bottles of Pinot Noir on the wall" all the way. At least that part
would have been fun. But he'd gotten a call a couple of days ago
from Sonny Chess, his "marketing counterpart." Chess had
suggested that he and George could really get to know each
other flying cross-country together and without really waiting
for George to agree had arranged for that to happen. Now the

Stellar and Circular marketing gurus would have quality time together. It was to be a bonding kind of thing. "I'll take care of it," Chess told him.

So instead of the direct flight to SFO from EWR, which was twenty-five minutes from the Beckers' residence, Chess had a car service pick George up at home and drive him, during morning rush hour, to JFK all the way out in Queens. Chess had to know George's address to have given it to the car service, but maybe his knowledge of geography was not so good. He probably remembered from elementary school that New Jersey was a separate state from New York. Or maybe he just didn't give a crap how inconvenient this was for George. Sonny knew that *he* was staying near JFK, so he had George fly out of there too, eating up entire hours he could have had to himself, at home.

Chess was an Elite Member of the frequent flyers clubs of several airlines, so he'd waited in the United Elite Club Lounge, being pampered, until George arrived. By that time they had to board the flight. The good news: Chess had gotten them both into first class for both legs of the flight, since now they had to change planes in Denver. The bad news: the bonding progress had been mediocre at best, so far, what with that schlep to Queens in the morning, turbulent air over the Rockies and a long delay in Denver. On the first leg of the trip Chess drank little bottles of Johnnie Walker as fast as the solicitous flight attendant could deliver them. He offered her his Corporate Platinum American Express Card to pay for his Scotches and George's Diet Cokes, but she reminded him that all the drinks in First Class were free. *Of course they were.* Bright sunlight streaming through the window glinted off the prestigious piece of plastic, catching George in the eye.

Now they sat on barstools at Chef Zimmy's Sports and Spirits near the G gates at Denver International. Clearly, Chess was destined to become George's next boss unless something changed the trajectory of life. Suppressing the emotions that this engendered – resentment over what felt like a demotion, extreme discomfort whenever he thought about having to report to someone who was young enough to have been one of his ninth grade students back in the day – George tried his best to like this silly, self-important, too-cool-for-school doofus. If there were to be a future for him as he hoped and maybe believed, he would have to find a way to get along with these people.

He could do it. George Becker could get along with anyone. Almost anyone.

Their flight delayed, they sat, and they drank, and they tried to get to know one another. It wasn't easy. Chess affected a Frank Zappa facial hair look, droopy moustache and underlip soul patch. His eyeglass frames were round and glowed a lime green. Unlike his face, his head was shaved. The overall effect was troubling; it prevented George from making good eye contact with him.

They'd been there an hour longer than the original flight schedule had predicted, and they had another extra hour delay, at least, before they could board the flight to Sacramento. George was trying his best and, to be fair, Chess was being amiable as well. It was clear that the younger man was intelligent and had at least enough empathy to recognize the minefield of potential problems inherent in the situation. Nevertheless, George was beginning to fear an awkward silence that could descend when they would run out of non-controversial topics. He worked himself into a zone comfortable enough to relate a Bert-and-Ernie anecdote which might amuse young Mr. Chess (he wasn't sure when he'd be able to feel comfortable calling him "Sonny"). Then maybe Chess would trot out some legendary old music biz tales.

He began with the misadventure of Bert's son Dougie's arrest for grand theft station wagon, featuring a high speed chase, half the complement of Jersey State Troopers, and Ashton Hartock getting drafted to go and bail him out; from there he segued into the story of the time that George and a couple of co-conspirators had managed to send Lane Coutell on a trip to visit a big, important, but, sadly, fictional new customer in Cleveland. "We told him, 'You're the only one Bert and Ernie trust enough to close this deal,'" George said, giggling a little at the memory. "That was the line that clinched it."

He could see that Chess was enjoying the story, so he tried not to embellish it too much. But before he could go on he saw a look of amazement sweep across Sonny's face. "What's—" George began to ask when he was interrupted. A pair of unmistakably feminine hands covered his eyes; a very familiar feminine voice whispered huskily in his ear, "Guess who?" Her aroma was subtle, dazzling and effective.

"Give me a hint," George said, stalling while his memory analyzed the data.

"You're breaking my heart!" the mystery woman pouted. "And you, you said you were my—"

He interrupted her and spun on his seat. "Rayne!" It was indeed Rayne Winters. He hugged her like an old friend. Although they weren't really *friend* friends, like come-over-for-pizza-and-TV friends, the ultra-famous two time-Academy Award-winning actress-turned-workout mogul had retained a real liking for George, crediting him with being partly responsible for sales of her first *Winters Wonder Workout* video taking off in New York, after which it blitzed the rest of the country, in no time flat becoming the first really huge money-making direct-to-video hit, all the way back in 1982. While he was glad to accept the accolades from her, and he had indeed busted his butt to promote it at Looney Looie's, he felt the credit was exaggerated. But he had learned over the years that modesty was an overrated virtue.

Rayne Winters turned her attention to the gob-smacked, weird-bearded Chess. "Do you know what this man did?" she asked him, running her long fingers through George's hair. "This sweet, young, handsome man put up a huge stage — in the middle of Times Square! For me! And we did a workout with a bunch of my gym rats and some celebs, and he had it projected on the big Jumbo-whatever-you-call-it, the giant sign, and the rest is history!" Her enthusiasm was invigorating, if exaggerated. "Even crazy old Mayor Koch put on striped tights and worked out! It was on every morning news show *in the world*," she enthused, "and we sold more videos than we could make! We sold *out* of them!"

"I remember seeing that on TV," Chess marveled, pulling his eyes away from Rayne Winters to look at George. "*You* did that?"

"Who's this guy, George, you sweetheart of a man? Did Bert and Ernie get you a new assistant? An amanuensis?"

"Rayne, this is Sonny Chess. He works for Circular Rec—I mean Circular Media."

Her face took on a look of concern. "Oh, shit," she said, "that's right. I heard that you guys had been bought out, right?"

She shook the younger man's hand and looked him up and down. "Sonny Chess from Circular Media, you are very lucky to be apprenticing with George Becker. He is a marketing genius and a remarkable human being."

If Rayne Winters were not *so* famous, this whole encounter might look like a set-up to fluff George up in front of his new soon-to-be boss. But for all the clever marketing contrivances George had concocted in his career, he could never have invented such a perfectly timed meeting.

To his credit, Sonny Chess just said, "I know."

"Good," she answered. "Now I'll allow you to buy me a Stolichnaya, neat."

The Rayne Winters promotion at the Loonie Looie's flagship store had been a high point for George. Five years later, when Bert and Ernie cashed out, selling their retail operation to the new, rapidly expanding chain of mega-video stores, Gangbusters Entertainment, the signed posters and the customized sweatbands from that event and the binders full of newspaper articles were some of George's favorite keepsakes.

George couldn't stop smiling. They all three moved to a booth near the back of the bar, a maneuver during which Rayne had to stop twice to satisfy autograph-seekers. Then she politely but firmly told the next one that she needed to "spend a little quality time with my boyfriend and his butler. You understand." The new round of drinks arrived as Rayne checked out the latest pictures of Will and Sally.

"What are you working on?" George asked her.

"Stuff," she said, with a dismissive wave. "Shit, to be honest. You wouldn't believe what happens to women when they hit forty in my business." A perfectly timed pause. "Never mind fifty."

"That's a shame," Chess said. "The world is waiting for *Star Girl Two*."

George rolled his eyes. *Sonny-boy is an asshole after all*, he thought.

Rayne skewered Sonny with a deadly spiked glare.

"I am an idiot," he said, trying to recover, but failing. "I didn't mean… I just didn't…"

She blew him off and turned to George. "What are *you* working on?" she asked him. "You're still married, I'll bet, to the lovely, brilliant Professor Alice May."

When George nodded, she pulled her fake pouty-face again. "You're still married too, Miss Winters," he said.

"Darn," she said. "You are right." Perfect pause. "For now."

"We were talking about practical jokes," Chess said.

She pretended not to hear him, so George jumped in. He was going to have to rescue the guy from himself. "Yeah," he said, and he gave a quick summary of the sending-Lane-to-Cleveland story.

She laughed appreciatively. Then she told them about filming *Tony and Toni*, a very heavy drama in which her character falls in love with an illiterate man whom she is teaching to read, played by Al Pacino. She told them that while they were shooting one of the heaviest scenes in the movie, Pacino, off-camera, had mooned her.

"We tried, but we couldn't get back on track and we lost a whole day of shooting. The director was pissed, but they were lucky to get Al in that picture in the first place. I didn't really know him too well back then. Everybody thinks he's always soooo serious, and they tiptoe around him, so that day he made everybody relax." She took another sip. "Not that it matters, but he has a very ugly ass."

When another round, or perhaps two, had been consumed, Sonny offered a story. George would never forget it.

"The worst practical joke ever was — well, I can't tell you the person's name, because—"

George and Rayne both cried foul. "Bullshit, Sonny-Boy," Rayne said. "We named names. Don't be a fucking weasel."

Chess was blushing through his soul patch, but he had gotten himself into it and he couldn't get out. "Okay. Okay. So, my boss, Jesse, he—"

"Full name," Rayne insisted.

"My boss, Jesse Powell-Portersmith—"

"A made up name!" Rayne protested, but George verified it. Chess continued to tell the story in which Powell-Portersmith had fired Circular's national sales manager for classical music. Sonny was in the office at the time, squirming and making matters worse for poor old Henry Salter, a quiet fellow, about forty years old, who had worked there for a decade.

"In the end, Henry left the office, took a few things, like the pictures on his desk, I guess, and headed out into the parking lot. It's a huge parking lot and his car must have been at the far end. Jesse – remember, he's my boss – is watching from his office window. He says to me, 'It's like the fucking Bataan Death March.'"

"Nice guy," George said. "But I thought you were gonna tell us about a practical joke."

"Well, that's the thing," Chess said. "Jesse says to me, 'Go out there and bring him back before he kills himself.'" He hesitated. He lifted his glass for a sip, but there was nothing in it, so he went on. "Firing him *was* the joke. He wasn't really fired."

Rayne and George were silent. Finally, George said, "You mean, he pretended to fire him?"

Rayne said, "He *fake fired* him?"

"Yeah," Chess said. He must have started to realize how not-funny the joke was to his audience. "I ran out there and got him. I told him it was okay, that Jesse just, well, he has a sick kind of sense of humor. Jesse wanted me to bring Henry into his office, I guess he was gonna apologize. Or something. But Henry wouldn't go to Jesse's office, and Jesse got busy and never got around to talking to Henry. It was a Tuesday. Henry gave two weeks notice on Friday."

It was silent again.

Rayne said, "You mean…" but she couldn't finish her sentence.

"It was pretty mean," Chess said, shaking his head, like a father relating one of his impish son's misdeeds, with a *What-are-you-gonna-do?* kind of shrug.

When George finally got his voice back, he said, "That wasn't… that wasn't funny. I mean, objectively, there's no joke there."

"I know, I know," Chess said. "It was sort of theater of the absurd. That was at least five or six years ago, and people still talk about it."

"I don't think you are using the right words," Rayne said. She spoke to him slowly as if she were addressing a dim-witted child. "That is not what the term 'theater of the absurd' means. What you just described is simple sadism." Chess opened his mouth to speak again, probably to agree with her, but George, unable to bear the sight of Chess making matters even worse, spoke first.

"You don't prank down, man." He felt sure that, if this was going to be a bad career move, to criticize his soon-to-be new boss in front of a famous movie star, it still had to be said, and he had to say it. Chess looked like he didn't understand.

George repeated himself. Then he added, "You prank *up*. You prank *across*." He was indicating levels and relationships between jokesters and those who would be the butts of those jokes, using the flat of his hand to describe the flow of interpersonal power. "You don't prank *down*."

Rayne tried to explain it to him. "People do it in my business all the time. That town is full of bullies. But even the biggest asshole bully sadist in Hollywood doesn't think it's a practical joke to dump on somebody who's below you on the org chart. It's just abuse of power. Like pinching a secretary's ass. I'll bet your Porterhouse does that too."

At that moment they heard the announcement that their flight was finally going to board in fifteen minutes. George and Sonny stood, but Rayne wasn't done expressing umbrage. "That classical music guy should have sued your funny boss. He probably still can! I'll bet the statute of limitations isn't up yet. What was his name again? Henry? Sonny, you should do the right thing. Get in touch with Henry and help him find a good employment attorney to sue the bastard."

Sonny said nothing, and Rayne didn't say goodbye. To George, she said, "Give me a call. I'll write you the best letter of recommendation. I still have some clout you know, even if I'm not thirty anymore."

"Thanks, Miss— I mean, thanks, Rayne. And you're more beautiful and sexy and talented now than when you were young. I mean, younger."

"That is pure BS young man, and I don't believe a word of it, but I'll take it anyway." She gave him one more hug and a kiss right on the lips. "Say hello to that darling Alice May and your sweet children."

"I will, and that reminds me. She gives you credit for teaching Sally to count."

"Me? When did I do that?"

"Alice May always worked out to your tape. Still does sometimes. And the baby would crawl around on the floor pretending to be exercising, too."

Rayne beamed.

"She would count along with you, '1, 2, 3, 4, 5, 6, 7, 8!' Of course the only problem was that she thought the next number was '...again' instead of 'nine.'"

EACH ATTENDEE HAD HIS OR HER OWN ROOM AT THE Velvet Vineyard Conference Centre in the tiny farming town of St. Helena, but the word "room" was a misnomer that failed to encompass their accommodations. They were in villas, and each villa contained only two living spaces, each of which consisted of a master bedroom with a king-sized bed, a living room with hand carved furniture from local artisans, a small but modern kitchen area, and a bathroom the size of the entire room he'd last stayed in at a Holiday Inn. The bathroom featured a giant tub in case you wanted to swim short laps, and two showers, one indoors and one outside. There was a fireplace in every living room and every bedroom; there were also terraces and patios. Some of the terraces had hot tubs or outdoor firepits, with plenty of local *piñon* split, stacked and ready to provide a soothing warmth, an invigorating aroma and a magical glow. *Man, these people are freaking firebugs!* Checking in after the second leg of their flight (during which he was able to tinker with his presentation on his laptop; the after-effects of too much Johnny Walker and a case of foot-in-mouth disease had done its job on Chess), George was taken by golf cart to his individual villa. Inside, beside the already mentioned amenities, the first thing George found was an envelope addressed to him on the mantle above the fireplace. In it was a welcome letter signed by Arthur Fishbein, Brian Fallow and a few of the other top executives who had arrived a day ago. The letter thanked him (as Angela Crofut had already done three weeks earlier) for his willingness to be a team player, and welcomed him to the incredibly challenging but equally exciting business at hand: Phase Two of the Integration of the Company.

The next thing George found was a pile of merchandise on the enormous bed. There was a cable knit sweater with a small, discreet Columbia Records insignia on the sleeve. There was a little "Shaggy is BOOMBASTIC!" mini-boom box, with a note identifying it as a gift to the east coast members from Arthur Fishbein. There were several baseball caps with logos of bands or albums or record companies; a navy blue pair of Meat Loaf jogging shorts (*as if that lard-ass ever jogged a day in his life*, George thought) that had the phrase "I Would Do Anything for Love" written on the front in white block letters, and "... but I Won't Do That" across the butt; a wristwatch with a picture of the lead singer of Hootie and the Blowfish and the name of their hit, "Time," across the center of his face; a shot glass from Jimmy Buffet's Margaritaville saloon chain and a martini glass left over from Blondie's '70s hit album *Heart of Glass*. *That one might be worth money*, George thought. There was an actual quarter-size crash test dummy promoting the band The Crash Test Dummies; and a globe of the world in the shape of a smashed in pumpkin promoting The Smashing Pumpkins' 1976 hit song, "1979." And there were CDs. Lots and lots, maybe forty CDs. They were mostly new, current releases – George noticed a Bruce Springsteen CD that he knew had not been released in stores yet. Each one had a tiny hole drilled through the upper right corner of the jewel case marking them as giveaways, but otherwise they were fine. Among them George found to his delight a Greatest Hits album from Dire Straits, with two of his favorite songs, "Sultans of Swing" and "Money for Nothing."

He called the front desk and asked for Stacy's room. "Hello, Stellar Vid– I mean Circular Media, Stacy speaking."

George asked her, "Do you believe all this shit? And all the CDs?"

"I know," said the ad director. "Hey, they didn't give you the Mariah Carey 'Always Be My Baby' baby doll sleep shirt and the Dr. Dre 'Nuthin' but a G Thang' G-string, did they?"

"No, but I got a "WHOOMP! There It Is" banana hammock. Did you get the Blondie martini glass?"

"Yeah. I'm not sure, but I think I'm a little shocked about the G-string thing. I'm going to tuck it away just in case I ever feel like filing a sexual harassment lawsuit. Did you get the Coolio "Gangsta's Paradise" cigarette case?"

"No. Tupac rolling papers?"

"Yep. Did you get the autographed Jimi Hendrix guitar?"

"*No!* Oh, you're fucking around, I get it."

"You caught me."

"This is wild isn't it?"

"Don't get seduced, George. You know that you tend to be a paranoid-in-reverse."

"I'm not getting seduced, Stace," George assured her. "I'm just saying that I think they've got better *tchotchkes* in the record business than we do in video, that's all. I'm just saying."

"They get CDs and *tchotchkes*, we get screeners and *tchotchkes*. What's the difference?"

"Yeah, well, I know, but this is a lot of stuff," George said. "That's all."

"It's not like they paid a nickel for any of it." Stacy said. "It's all promo shit from the labels."

"I realize that."

"You did the very same thing last year in Montego Bay at the National Sales Meeting, remember? And your stuff was better."

"I guess so," George said.

"In fact, I'll bet that's where they got the idea."

"You think, really?"

"George, quit selling yourself short. You're better and smarter than they are. I am too."

"You're right."

"I gotta go, I gotta call home. I'll see you at..." he could tell that she was consulting the printed schedule of events that was in all of their rooms. "See you at the "Welcome Cocktail Party." It's at seven o'clock. *Seven?* Christ, that means we won't sit down to eat until nine, and that will be midnight for us. How fucking stupid and inconsiderate these people are."

"You're right," he said again.

"I'll come by in an hour and we'll go find a little *nosh*, okay?"

"Okay, bye."

George called home too. Alice May was scheduled to get home that same day from Chicago where she'd been giving a speech and promoting her new book, which was actually the seventh revised edition of *A Knotted String: A History of Preliterate Peoples of Western South America*. To their amazement, *A Knotted String* had become something of a classic in the world of textbooks, having been adopted by anthropology departments at colleges and universities around the world, providing them with a perennial "extra" income stream for the last several years. The title referred to a remarkable method of record-keeping and communication used by certain tribes who had no written form of language, no alphabet. Just *quipus*, knotted strings.

Sally answered. "Mom's landed and she's on her way home, should be here soon. Where are you again? I mean, sorry, but you guys are getting harder to keep track of these days."

That tickled George. "Why does that sound like something moms and dads say to their kids rather than the other way around?"

"Sorry, I don't mean—"

"No, don't be sorry. You're right. It's a perfectly valid statement." He told her where he was, and why.

"Right, oh right. I knew that," Sally said. "Mom told me…"

George recognized the hesitation in her voice. "What?"

"Nothing. Well, I guess it's funny. Mom told me that what was happening at your work, with the two companies eating each other and all… She said it was like the *Taínos* and the *Caribs* in the islands. You know, conquering, savagery, the whole nine yards."

"I guess so, I guess that's… a pretty good analogy," George said. It had never occurred to him that Alice May would use an anthropological metaphor to explain to Will or Sally the internecine warfare involved in his current job situation. She had never used that metaphor with him. Thinking about it, though, it was apt.

"I think Mom's taxi is pulling up now. Anyhow, if it makes you feel any better, I think all that stuff about the *Caribs* eating their enemies was bullshit, just PR. Of course if the *Taínos* believed the *Caribs* were cannibals, then I guess it served its purpose."

"Thanks, sweets. I'll keep that in mind during the next battle. What do you want me to bring you from California?"

"Daddy, I'm fifteen. You don't have to keep buying me a present whenever you go away on a business trip."

"Okay, thanks. Good to know," he said.

"No prob. See you when you get here. Here's Mom."

She gave the phone to Alice May who said, "Daddy's girl is growing up."

He told Alice May that he missed her very much, which he did, and he learned that her trip was "fine." Sally took the phone back from her mother. "Daddy, your new company sells CDs now too, right?"

"Right."

"Okay, well you don't have to buy me any presents, but if there are any CDs just lying around by, like, you know, Tracy Chapman or the Gin Blossoms or Outkast or the BoDeans or anybody like that, you could bring those home if there's room in your suitcase."

"Smashing Pumpkins? Seal? Bone Thugs-n-Harmony?"

"Ooh, listen to Daddy getting all hip and gangsta."

"What, no Beatles or Bob Dylan?"

"Don't need to ask for those, you'll bring them home anyway."

"Good point. I'll see what I can do."

"Thanks Daddy. I love you. Here's Mom again."

When Alice May got back on the line he said, "You're raising an anthropologist in your own image."

"She's in your image too," she said.

"She sure is smart," he said, and Alice May agreed.

"Remember how she would play with the *quipus* when she was little, and ask me about them? Now she makes them, and she doesn't go anywhere without wearing little stringy bracelets that she makes on her ankles or wrists. Next she'll be selling them in the cafeteria."

"So, everything went well?" he asked her, hoping for more specific good news about the trip to Chicago, the presentation, the speech. He'd been working very hard to suppress anger about the fact that he would have wanted to be there... But this hot mess here was his job, he knew.

"Better than that," she answered. "I'll tell you all about it when you get home."

That was their signal for getting off the phone. "Good," he said. "Great."

"What?" she asked. He must've sounded like something was on his mind.

"Nothing," he said. "Just... What is a 'paranoid-in-reverse'?"

Alice May chuckled. "Who called you that?" she wanted to know.

"Why do you think... Um, Stacy did."

"Yeah, she knows you, George. A paranoid-in-reverse is a person who thinks that other people are plotting to make him happy."

STACY WAS RIGHT, OF COURSE. MOST OF THE Stellarites were exhausted and yawning by the time they could gracefully escape dinner and head to their beds. Not George, though; he was way too keyed up. The presentations were tomorrow, and he wanted to look over his one more time – maybe practice it a couple of times. He'd done hundreds of presentations of all kinds, but never with PowerPoint before, and he had in fact just taught himself the software in order to make the best possible impact at this meeting. Really, what he wanted was simply to make a positive impression. When he got back to his room there were fresh, brand new "Rhythm of the Night" pajamas laid out for him, and amazingly, a book of Buddhist, Christian, Jewish and Muslim prayers and words of wisdom, wrapped in a leather book cover with a picture of the singer Jewel, and the words "Who Will Save Your Soul?" George tossed it all aside, showered and climbed into bed, eschewing the promotional jammies. He reread the presentation, once silently and once out loud. His idea was not to memorize it, but simply to be so familiar with it that he could deliver it comfortably, almost as if he were speaking extemporaneously.

"All right," he said aloud. "Enough already." Reaching for the lamp by the bed he noticed the prayer book and picked it up. There, on the title page, was Jewel's autograph and a message that gave him pause. *Dear George, Have a great time in California, but who will save your soul? Your friend, Jewel.*

BEAUTIFUL MORNING SUNLIGHT FLOODED THE GLASS-walled conference room where the actual business meetings were to take place. They all arrived right on time, at eight am. There were fresh flowers on the long mahogany conference table, name cards in front of all the seats which were obviously assigned, and coffee, tea, fresh-squeezed orange, grapefruit and papaya juices, Coke, Diet Coke, and two kinds of bottled water laid out, as well as some sad west coast excuses for bagels, croissants, and muffins. Along with the eating and drinking there was much greeting and mutual welcoming and introducing for about fifteen minutes.

George (and, no doubt, the rest of the Stellarites) was absolutely amazed when he was introduced to the VP of Purchasing, but he immediately learned why he was known as "Staples." Up until then, if he thought about it at all, he just assumed that Charles "Staples" Opatashu used to work for the office superstore chain. But that wasn't it at all. Staples only had hair in a narrow path down the center of his skull, and every bit of it was gathered into a series of about a dozen spikes, the longest of which stuck up a good six inches from the top of his head. That one was the yellow of Bart Simpson's skin. Each of the others was also dyed a color not normally found in nature. When the eye was able to withdraw from this remarkable sight, it traveled down to Staples' actual face, the seven or eight shiny adornments of which were what gave him his name, not his former place of employment. If George had been in charge of nicknames, Staples would have been named Bull instead, after the ring which passed through his septum and protruded from both nostrils, and which absolutely begged for a leash to be attached to it so he could be led out to the pasture to service Farmer Brown's cow. Upon introduction, Staples smiled and shook George firmly by the hand. "I can't wait to learn all about the buying on the video side from you guys. From everything I've heard, your team is the best in the business. I'd like to go ahead and set up a phone appointment with you. When do you think you'd be able to do that?"

George was speechless, shocked by the young man's appearance, shocked by the unexpectedness of seeing this apparition in a high level executive meeting, but most shocked by the normal (for Californians), mature, intelligent-sounding voice that came out of the frightening face in front of him. Making matters even stranger, the act of smiling and speaking revealed further metallic adjustments to nature's original design, modifying not only Staples' tongue but also five of the teeth on the top row in front. George was rescued from his vocal paralysis when Angela Crofut banged her water glass with a spoon and suggested that "we all go ahead and find out seats."

Fallow kicked it off with a joke so lame that even his minions' forced laughter sounded half-hearted at best. This was a man so humorless that his ersatz laughter set George's teeth on edge.

Fallow gave an even more intense version of his Integration Speech. He went so far as to warn everyone in the room that he knew that in these situations, there were always resentments, jealousies, grudges, competitiveness, even outright non-cooperation and sabotage. There was some level of occurrences of this type in most buyout scenarios, he said, on both sides, and everyone could tell that he knew what he was talking about not only from reading articles on the subject in management publications, but from real world experience. He was not accusing anyone of anything, he said, but if such were to occur, he wanted to be notified immediately. When he said "on both sides," he made eye contact with almost every single Circularian around the table. George caught Fat Mack's eye, Fat Mack nodded without moving his tremendous head at all, and each of the other Stellarites, with the possible exception of Lane, who never took his eyes off of Fallow, also gave each other a look.

Fallow introduced Arthur Fishbein, who stood and made as if to walk to the head of the table, thought better of it, and just leaned on the table in front of him. "I want every single person in this room to know something. None of you has worked for this company before today. Not you, Richie," he said to little Vinograd, whose eyes seemed always to be glittering with hot angry tears under his unibrow. "Not you, Lydia, or you, George." He looked at Lydia when he said her name, and she made a silent little huffing exhalation through her nose, a facial gesture that her colleagues were quite familiar with; people who didn't know her well wouldn't even notice the slight nostril flaring. And he looked right at Fat Mack when he said George's name, which amused the entire east coast contingent and about half the west coast one. Vinograd, and Lane, and Jacques-Francois and Sonny Chess each kept a straight face, locked tightly on Fishbein, who was as oblivious to the mistake he had made as he was to the identities of some of his new employees. "Not Brian, or Sonny, or Angela. Not even me, either." He paused for dramatic effect. "Some of you used to work for a fairly successful music one-stop called Circular Records. That company went out of existence several weeks ago. Some of you east coast types–" he waved his arm vaguely in the direction of George, though the Stellarites and the Circularians were intentionally interspersed all around the table. "You used to work for another company that ain't around no more, an outstanding company with an outstanding record of profitability in the video industry.

"Not any more. Everyone in this room works for a different company now, and it's called Circular Media, Incorporated. It has a brand new logo that Sonny will unveil this week at these meetings, and that logo looks like neither Stellar Video's old logo, nor Circular Records' old logo. The management structure is different. Brian will be going over all this stuff– When Brian, tomorrow?"

"Tomorrow and Thursday, Arthur," said Fallow helpfully.

"Tomorrow and Thursday he'll be doing that. Even the goals of the company are different from those of the two old, no-longer-existent companies.

"Now one last thing, and I want all of you, especially those of you in the video division of Circular Media who don't know me yet, to listen to me very carefully." He leaned farther forward toward the middle of the table, supporting himself with his fists on the table; from this position he craned his neck as far as it would go from left to right, eyeballing everyone except the two people seated on either side of him, whom he could no longer see from where he was. He lowered his voice, but he spoke quite clearly as he did his very best to get his message through to every person there.

"Every single person in this room has been chosen, by me, because I feel that you are the best possible person to be doing the job to which you are or will be assigned. I don't want to lose a single one of you, and I will fight to keep any and every one of you. And I always get what I fight for. We are in this together. It's ours to win or lose. The best talent in the business is assembled here in this room. All we really have to do is want to win."

Fishbein sat down heavily in his chair, took a handkerchief from his pocket, and blew his nose impressively. There was no other sound in the room. Then Lane Coutell clapped. He only clapped once though, because no one joined him. And then they continued the meeting.

Fallow went over the schedule for the next three days, giving them all a little idea of what to expect. The Circularians in the room had all been to these events before; none of the Stellarites except Killian, who had worked for Paramount Pictures years before, had ever done anything like it. The whole thing fascinated George. The rest of the morning was given over to priority-setting, the aim of which was to identify three things. First, they would go ahead and tease out the *low-hanging fruit*; that is, those opportunities that were most ripe, easiest to reach, and most likely to be successful in the near term. Next they would try to designate the *footballs*, those projects which, if they were marshalled down the field effectively and with great teamwork, could be kicked through the goal posts before the fourth quarter whistle blew. And finally they were to go ahead and determine the *blue sky goals*; in order to do this they had to *take the 30,000 foot view*, think so far outside the box that they couldn't see the box, and not be afraid to *dream big*.

They broke up into groups of three and four people, with some Stellarites and some Circularians in each group. Each group was given tools: a roll of masking tape, a huge pad of newsprint sheets the size of movie posters, and a red, a green, and a blue magic marker. Over the next hour they went through a process of proposing ideas, trying to agree about which of the three aforementioned categories the ideas fell into, and finally prioritizing them within those categories, ranking their likelihood of successful completion and their potential dollar value. They brainstormed, they kicked things around, they butted heads. They went ahead and did the assignment. When the hour was almost up they tore down all the pages they had put on the glass walls. Then the neatest writer in the group, summed it all up on one poster.

One group member was appointed to present the ideas to the whole gathering of minds. Then they went around the room, and the presenters for each of the six groups read off their list of priorities, spoke a bit about why each was chosen, and fielded a few questions from the listeners. After each of the first five groups' presenters was done, there was polite applause.

Killian was the presenter for the last group to go, and he managed to deliver his group's ideas while at the same time getting laughs by interweaving jokes and insults, first about himself, then he nailed Bert Jacobs, then some of the Stellarites there in the room. George was worried that Killian was having too much fun, that he might go too far, might get down on his knees and do his impression of little Richie *à la* Toulouse Lautrec. Instead, he leaned on the table exactly as Fishbein had done only two hours earlier, lowered his voice an octave, and said, "You all work for a new company. And remember: piss me off and you'll need to find *another* new company to work for." The Stellarites in the room fell apart with helpless laughter, not so much over the joke, which wasn't particularly funny in any normal sense of the word, but over Killian's balls in having said it, right there, in that context. George tried to catch Sonny Chess' eye, to give him a wink at this fine, unplanned example of "pranking up, not down," but Sonny was oblivious. The Circularians were momentarily shocked into silence, but when they realized that Fishbein was laughing his fat ass off along with the east coasters, most but not all of them joined in too. Fishbein roared between guffaws, "Of course, he's right, it's true!" Killian's regular response to such audience approval was a mock look of confusion, as if to say "What? What did I say? Did someone say something funny?" which of course prolonged the laughter.

Finally, when everyone had settled down, Fallow led them all in an exercise, eliciting their avid participation, in which they combined and folded together and cooked each of the six sets of priorities down into one final set of priorities, which he wrote on one giant sheet of newsprint.

Fallow congratulated them. They had now set the goals for Circular Media for the next three months, the next year, and the next three years. George was ultimately a little baffled as to how some of the priorities got on the final list, but most of them made *some* kind of sense. Still, it reminded him of a card trick that his father used to do when George was little, where he would manipulate George into selecting just the card that he wanted him to, and then congratulated *him* on working the magic.

Finally it was lunchtime and they all took a break to eat,

pee, walk around, stretch, and mingle. Fat Mack asked George in a low voice how his group had worked. "Not too bad, I guess," George replied. "What about yours?"

"I'll tell you, it seemed very open and democratic and all, and yet when it was done, I felt like it had all happened without me."

"I think I know what you mean. I kind of felt that way also."

Lunch ended, they returned to the Crystal Conference Room, and the presentations began. First Richie Vinograd gave his operations overview. He showed chart after chart that showed to the tenth of a cent how much it cost to do every single function in the company from shipping one CD to processing one order, factoring in every conceivable resource and expense, both monetary and non-monetary. George found it interesting – he'd never thought all this stuff through to the penny, and he wondered if Ernie or Bert ever had. Vinograd used a long wooden pointer to draw their attention to specific points on his graphs, and, incredibly, not a single person in the room laughed, despite the facts that only a small part of Vinograd could be seen above the table. When he needed to point at the items near the top of the screen, he had to sort of wave the pointer in their general direction, because even with his arm extended and a three-foot pointer he didn't come close. It was an amazing performance.

Fourteen presentations in total were on the agenda for the afternoon, seven more before the three forty-five coffee break, and six after it. Of course, every single presentation went at least five or more minutes longer than the allotted time. Sonny Chess gave the music marketing presentation, using many of PowerPoint's most "creative" features. Words went flying across the screen accompanied by the sound of jet engines, a graph depicting a slow first half of the year was indicated by an anthropomorphic line that fell dejectedly off the chart and crashed, accompanied by the sound of breaking glass. Of course he ended on a triumphant note with his marketing department, which functioned as a pseudo separate company under the sobriquet CircularLogic, beating last year's numbers by more than 15%, an amazing accomplishment against all odds. His final slide exploded onto the screen with the words

CircularLogic
WE ROCK CIRCULAR MEDIA'S WORLD!
Today, Tomorrow, and Beyond!

This was the act George had to follow. Finally. He strode to the front of the room as Sonny returned to his place, and the latter gave George an exaggeratedly macho handshake.

"Good job," George said to him.

"Rock on," Sonny said back.

George looked at everyone and said "Good afternoon." Before he could say anything else, he noticed Arthur Fishbein, who was directly across the table at the far end. Fishbein had fallen asleep and his head, rather than falling forward onto his bosomy chest, instead lolled backward at nearly a right angle. His mouth was open wide, and his whole body was bobbling in response to its own arhythmic snoring. What made it all the more surreal was the fact that every single person in the room was pretending that they were unaware of this, although the snores by now sounded, at least to George, like special effects from *The Exorcist*. George managed to unlock his attention from this startling sight and sound and nodded to Jacques-Francois who was queuing up the video marketing presentation in the computer. The first slide came on. It was an image of a movie theater marquee displaying a title: THE FUTURE. George smiled and looked at the Frenchman to click to the next slide; that was when the bulb in the overworked projector exploded with a distinct pop accompanied by an acrid odor and a rising contrail of purple smoke.

As an "Ohhhh" oozed from the group, Jacques-Francois turned off the projector and leapt into action. "Not to worry, Zhorzh," he said in his accent, which, though it might have sounded lovely in another context, seemed jarringly out of place now. "We always have a spare!" He ran to the back of the room where the carrying cases were piled and returned in short order with the promised new bulb. Courageously, he removed the broken one with his bare hands despite the fact that it was red hot and jagged, and fanned the inside of the machine with his notepad to cool it down. Then he popped the new one in, waited a moment, and turned it back on.

Nothing happened.

Jacques-Francois, Fallow, Powell-Portersmith and Chess gathered around the thing and leered into it, discussing and pointing like a quartet of auto mechanics consulting under the hood of a problematic vehicle. Even Fishbein woke, at least for a minute.

"I am vairy sawry to have to report," the Frenchman finally announced to the group, "that the hit of the bilb" – heat of the bulb – "has burnt up the circuitry. This mah-shin" – machine – "will not work again today. Pair haps not eh-vair." He bowed his head as if he had just delivered last rites to a comrade in the fields of Verdun.

After a great deal of hubbub, George took the bull by the horns and insisted on giving his presentation without the use of the computer slide show. "I have copies of everything here," he said, indicating his folder, "and if something absolutely must be seen to be understood, well, I'll just pass it around." The appreciative audience applauded his bravery and inventiveness in the face of travail and his show-must-go-on determination. George also dispensed with the microphone which the previous department heads had used, preferring to project his voice throughout the room from his diaphragm without electronic enhancement, as he had first learned to do back in his undergraduate dramatic phase.

He pointed to the totally blank screen and said, "As you can clearly see..." *See, Killian's not the only one capable of cracking a joke.* Fully cognizant of the fact that, with the delay caused by the projector fiasco it was now approaching five o'clock, George settled into his talk, and set a more accelerated pace than he would otherwise have chosen. He brought everyone up to speed on the funding streams for which marketing was responsible, explaining how positively this fiscal year's final results compared to those of the previous year. He gave a quick sketch of the financial instability of several of their competitors. Then he struck a cautionary tone, as he predicted a leveling off of video growth, the impending collapse of a number of supportive vendors, and the saturation of VCR penetration in the United States. This middle section of his talk was intended to demonstrate that George was knowledgeable about both the past and the future of his area of expertise and that he was not one to sugar coat bad news. In this way, he would set up the dramatic final section in which he illustrated the strategies necessary to outwit and avoid the perils of the maturing video marketplace, not merely to survive, but to thrive in the next phase of home entertainment, through clear vision and smart planning.

He began this part and made serious eye contact with key people around the room. "Fortunately–" He was looking at Fallow and to his initial shock and then near-panic saw that the CEO was giving him the impatient spinning finger "speed it up, let's go" signal, the one that said *Ok, come on, get it over with*. It was accompanied by Fallow's dead-eyed stare and what looked almost exactly like a sneer, though it could have been the man's attempt at a sympathetic smile.

George finished in a tumble of words of which he was unaware, and found himself back in his seat, as everyone else got up to take their coffee break more than an hour and a half late. He was pretty sure he had not simply stopped talking mid-sentence and sat down, but he had no clue what he had said. The only thing he was certain about was that he had not delivered the all-important final segment of his talk, and so in essence must have left his colleagues, none of whom could have seen Fallow's impatient gesture, with the impression that George had traveled three thousand miles to inform them all that the future was hopeless and that he had no idea what on earth could be done about it.

WHEN THE BREAK WAS OVER, THE GROUP QUICKLY agreed that it made the most sense to meet at a quarter to eight the next morning instead of the planned eight-thirty am start, and finish the remaining presentations then, canceling, if need be, one of the less than essential "team spirit activities" scheduled for Wednesday afternoon. Several people slapped George's back as they returned to their villas to wash and rest up before the evening's dinner, which was going to be sponsored jointly by Columbia Records and Columbia TriStar Home Video in a nice tip of the hat to the synergies waiting to be exploited by this new audio+video distribution company. George smiled numbly, afraid to make matters worse by whining about how unfair it all was.

Dinner began with a slick co-presentation by Dominick Castellano, Executive Vice-President for Domestic Distribution of Columbia Records and Stephen Abramowitz, Senior Vice-President and General Manager of Columbia TriStar Home Video. First both men took to the small stage that had been specially set up in the garden of the French Laundry, the famous restaurant that people had been anticipating going to since the schedule had first been circulated. Radiant heaters were stationed strategically around the area, changing the chilly autumn evening into a warm summer night. The honchos from Columbia took turns praising the accomplishments of Fishbein, Fallow, Powell-Portersmith, even Staples, as well as several of the former Stellar Video execs. George was aware that important, impressive, famous Steve Abramowitz, who was married to a starlet so beautiful that people were in awe of him for that accomplishment alone, had mentioned his name, had thanked him for his work in front of the whole group. Rather than being the icing on the cake of what should have been a glorious day, however, it was further reminder that the cake had been stolen, leaving nothing but sugary frosting.

They showed a ten-minute video promoting the exciting albums and concert tours, movies and TV events and other video projects, all of which would be coming out from the various arms of this multimedia conglomerate in the next twelve months alone. After the promotional clips came short, specially-filmed spots featuring famous entertainers, including Harrison Ford, Billy Crystal, Madonna, Boyz II Men, Julia Roberts, Michael Jordan, Macaulay Culkin, and ten members of the New York Rangers hockey team, in uniform, on the ice at Madison Square Garden. In each one, the Extremely Famous Person (except for the Rangers) sat in a black director's chair, looked at an unseen interviewer, praised the work of Circular Records and Stellar Video (only Julia Roberts had been induced to call it Circular Media) and thanked those gathered tonight for making what they did possible. Some of them finished by looking directly into the camera's lens and saying something either funny, teasing, or sincere directly to one or more of the people in the room. There was loud, appreciative applause and laughter when the tape ended, and the Columbia execs, looking pleased, assured them that they would all receive a copy of the video.

Dinner was more impressive than even the most hopeful of them had expected, including champagne toasts, and the most delicately filleted and broiled salmon that George had ever tasted. As a dessert that had to have been a collaboration between a pastry chef and an architect was being served, bright lights suddenly illuminated a section of the garden no one had noticed before. There was a stage there, bigger than the one Abramowitz and Castellano had used over on the other side, upon which was a large drum kit and a bunch of guitars and amplifiers. Dom Castellano kicked off "the evening's *actual* entertainment."

"I am proud to introduce Columbia Recording artists, The Rembrandts!" All but a few people looked at each other to see if anybody had heard of this band, as five young men ran onto the stage waving and grinning. Once the drummer had settled on his stool and the rhythm guitarist saw that the rest of his bandmates were ready, they slammed into a high energy, high volume performance of their hit song, "I'll Be There For You," better known as the theme from the TV situation comedy "Friends." Live, the fluffy, cutesy pop tune was transformed into a surprisingly kick ass rock and roll powerhouse, with a screaming guitar lead and a jazzy drum solo. The extended version climaxed with the final refrain. Everybody sang along with "I'll be there for you," and the band would answer with spoofy lines never heard on TV, like "When your pants start to fall!"

"I'll be there for you," bellowed the audience.

"When I'm nowhere at all!" answered the lead singer.

"I'll be there for you!"

"When you can't even crawl!"

"I'll be there for you!!"

"When you're ready to ball!!"

"I'll be there for you!!"[6]

And the band brought it right back down with the final line, "Cause you're there for me too," a little feedback and a stuttering drum finish. The audience jumped to its feet and showered these guys whom they hadn't known from Adam's housecat fourteen minutes earlier with raucous, appreciative applause.

The Rembrandts played a couple more tunes, then said goodnight and left to more warm applause. Someone somewhere made the next introduction, but it couldn't be heard over the still sizzling audience. But before the crowd could catch its breath and sit down again, Matthew Perry and Lisa Kudrow, the actors who played the two funniest characters on "Friends," came out. The Stellarites were more impressed than the Circularians, but everyone was knocked out. Jesse Powell-Portersmith, sitting at the table with George, Hock and Stacy, asked who they were and why they were there. Stacy explained who they were, and Hock pointed out that both of them, aside from being stars of the number one show on TV, had major starring roles in big budget movies opening before Christmas. George said nothing, but rolled his eyes in amazement that this guy, who would be in charge of all sales for an entertainment company, had so little awareness of what was going on. *That can't be good*, he thought.

Kudrow and Perry did a hilarious stand up routine, and roundly roasted their show, Columbia, the TV business, and the movies that their fellow cast members had already done which had bombed, especially the one that Matt "Joey" LeBlanc had made with a baseball-playing gorilla. Before it was over though, George had slipped away back to his room. It wasn't until the next morning that he heard about the solo acoustic Bruce Springsteen performance that had finished the evening's festivities.

They began the presentations the next morning while they had a quick continental breakfast. In order to save more time, the remaining department heads agreed to cut their talks down to their essentials. George took this as another slight to him. To make matters worse, Staples, the music buyer, colorful hair spikes and all, had somehow acquired a whole new projector for his PowerPoint presentation. George was insane with rage, which he bottled up somehow, like a cork in a volcano. No one noticed.

The freak finished, and Hock was next. He hadn't planned any visual aids, just a talk he had written out by hand on note cards. George's simmering fury abated slightly, as he remembered another time long ago that Hock had read from index cards with startling results, and he almost laughed at the thought. Over the intervening years Hakizimana Wasef had become the most knowledgeable, craftiest, sharpest buyer in the business. His friend's success now would ameliorate some of George's pain.

Hock looked at his first card, and smiled warmly at his audience. Then he looked at it again. Then he looked at the people in the room again. No one could have anticipated what came next: He smiled and said, "I can't do this." George's insides twisted in pain, seeing his friend, already a pessimist, stand in front of this group and act humble. Hock wasn't *humble*. George realized that Hock had never spoken in front of anything other than the B Team's lunch or breakfast gatherings, never stood up and addressed even the telemarketers' weekly meeting. Hock, who could manipulate the toughest studio rep, on the phone or in person, to give Stellar better terms than anyone in the business; who could bench press 255 pounds; who somehow supported his sister and his mother as well as his girlfriend and her daughter, couldn't do this. So he sat down.

People all began shouting encouragement. "You're among friends."

"You can do it."

"Take a deep breath."

"It's ok, relax and try again later."

For a moment he glanced at his cards again, and a few people said, "You're ok, don't worry." But then he looked up and smiled again, and just said, "Nope. Sorry," and remained seated.

Fallow finally stepped in to relieve the uncomfortable silence in the room and sent the next presenter up. George didn't catch a word anybody else said. And Hock, back in his seat, returned to listening and taking notes as he had been doing.

When the last presentation was blessedly finished there was a break, and all the Stellarites clustered together outside under the walnut trees. Hock was laughing, telling his friends not to worry about him. He didn't know until he got up there that it would be impossible for him to give his talk. He had suspected that it might be difficult. For one thing, his vision blurred the moment he stood up, and there was no way he could read the neatly lettered cards. Cubbage massaged Hock's shoulders.

Before the break ended, Cubbage showed George and Fat Mack Foley a picture, more like an editorial cartoon, that she had drawn in her notebook while pretending to take notes. It showed a big hammer smacking the top of a nail or a stake of some kind, pounding it through something that looked like a table. On closer examination he saw that the hammer was labeled "Fallow," the spike was labeled "Stellar," and the round table through which it was being forced had "Circular" written on the edge of it. Fat Mack began to laugh.

"Get it George?" he said. "It's Fallow trying to punch Stellar, a square peg, into Circular, a round hole. Good one, Ellen."

"Don't let anybody see that, Cubbage," George warned. "That's exactly the type of thing he was talking about."

"I already made *sure* one of them saw it," she said.

"Who?" George asked, worried.

"Why?" Fat Mack asked, curious.

"I made sure that little speck of birdshit, Vinograd, saw it. I pretended that I didn't know he saw it, but he'd been checking out my notes, and my tits, for two days. Imagine? That mosquito? He wouldn't know *what* to do with these. But that wasn't why. I figured 'What the hell?' and I looked over and glanced at *his* notes. He writes in this tiny scrawl, just like him. At first I couldn't make out much of what he had written. Then I saw that he had written the name of each person who was presenting, and then bullet pointed phrases after each name. He had written Hock's name and then, after Hock sat back down, he had scratched two thick pencil lines through his name. I looked back a minute later, and he had written in capital letters: STELLAR PEOPLE – NON-STARTERS. That's when I drew this and made sure he could 'accidentally' see it."

"Really?" Fat Mack Foley said.

"You're shitting me," George said.

"*Really*," Fat Mack repeated.

"Be cool, you guys," George said.

The break was over and they went back inside.

Fallow got up and gave them a list of options for the rest of the day. It was up to them, the Core Management Group (CMG), to determine the nature of the rest of the conference.

Ellen Cubbage still sat next to Richie Vinograd, and George and Fat Mack were almost directly across the table.

Vinograd gestured with his pencil without actually raising his hand. It was a slight, conservative gesture that would have seemed more appropriate in a small office with no more than three people present. He spoke, assuming he had been recognized.

"I've been thinking about it, and I really think we should all go ahead and– "

Those were the only words he got out. That was all it took. Only a handful of people in the room had any idea that the fuse had been lit half an hour ago, had been prepared in small, mean ways for weeks if not months, and that what they were now witnessing was the spark finally reaching the dry powder. If George or anyone else in the room for that matter lived to be a hundred years old, they would never lose the image of a bearded, three hundred-pound man screaming primally, climbing onto the conference table and dropping like an anchor, crushing Vinograd and his chair beneath him. It reminded George of a scene in *A Fish Called Wanda*, when stuttering, timid Michael Palin accidentally causes a piano to fall fifty feet and flatten an old lady's toy poodle. Cubbage, on Vinograd's left, nearly became collateral damage, but just barely got out of the way. Fearing the worst, ten people tried to grab onto the flailing arms of Fat Mack, but they were unable to stop the punishment the giant was doling out with his ham-sized fists. Those who tried to restrain him were tossed back into the others who were rushing into the fray. Angela Crofut was screaming bloody murder on the other side of the room, and bloody murder was exactly what George feared would be at least one of the charges Fat Mack would soon be facing. Killian got accidentally smacked by one of Foley's back swings. It bloodied his nose and rocked him back into Jacques-Francois who, fearing he was the next Circular person to be attacked for no reason at all by one of these insane video people threw an arm across Killian's neck and began choking him. Cubbage jumped onto Jacques-Francois' back and bit his ear.

George now didn't know which fight to try to stop, before it all became one big fight. But clearly the most immediate need was to rescue the quasi-midget if he were not already dead, to save Fat Mack from California's gas chamber, which Susan Sarandon had not been able to do for Sean Penn in *Dead Man Walking*. He tried again to stop the pounding of the huge fists. No one could move Foley, but finally little Stacy somehow succeeded in squirming between the giant and whatever was left of Vinograd, and a couple of the men were able to pull the victim out from under and rush him away.

Meanwhile, the other fight was verging on becoming a barroom brawl like the kind that would be in the next-to-last-scene of every comic western John Wayne ever starred in. George thought about perching on the conference table with a bottle and smashing it on whatever head rolled within reach, like Gabby Hayes must have done a hundred times. But this was no John Wayne movie, so instead he dove in and tackled Killian, and somebody else did the same to the Frenchman, and everybody was screaming "CUT IT OUT! STOP IT!" as loud as they could.

When it was over, two of the panes of the Crystal Conference Room were smashed. A leg of the conference table was splintered, and three chairs were shattered beyond recognition. George was not unhappy to notice that the recently acquired replacement projector had swan-dived off the table and committed suicide on the floor. The screen was hanging from the ceiling by only one corner.

Police cars were screaming into the parking lot.

Brian Fallow had a purple welt that half-closed his left eye. George had been impressed that such a skinny, bloodless individual had plunged fearlessly into the scrum, and he mentally gave him points for this. Vinograd, strapped to a gurney, was twitching as he was loaded into an ambulance, so presumably he still had a pulse. Cubbage had a bloody lip and her shirt was ripped; the tall Frenchman was also bleeding from the mouth as well as his ear. Lane was sitting in one of the remaining chairs, just holding his head. Hock and George looked at each other, surprised that they had received no apparent wounds. Sonny Chess was limping badly and his glasses were broken. Staples' hair spikes were all crushed. Stacy was sitting in a corner on the floor, finishing a brief cry. Most of the others had run outside in terror, first among them Jesse Powell-Portersmith, followed by several women.

Bloody-faced Dave Killian and Fat Mack Foley sat on the floor, propped up against a wall, side by side. Fat Mack Foley looked as if he were sitting on the beach, staring out to sea with a bent smile on his face. Dave Killian was giggling and shaking his head in wonder.

George and Hock went around checking on the wounded. Hock handed Fallow some paper towels to wipe his face, and helped him to his feet. Fallow thanked him. When Hock saw that he was stable on his feet, he said to him, "I guess you're going to go ahead and call this conference finished."

Chapter Thirteen
Integration Phase Three:
Disintegration

1997-
1998

AS EVER, WORD TRAVELS FAST, AND BAD NEWS AND juicy gossip travels fastest of all. When the Jersey City crew arrived at the office two days later, they were greeted with cheers. The theme from *Rocky* blasted over the intercom and souvenir mini-boxing gloves from *Raging Bull* were draped over the desk chairs of Killian, George, Stacy, Lane, Cubbage and Hock. A huge banner was hung across the entrance lobby that said, "OUR HEROES!" Nobody could get any work done that day, as the stories had to be told and retold.

Almost everyone gathered in Bert's old office, the so-called "guest office," to hear and tell the stories, including what had taken place back home as the news had spread. Terry Lunceford told them that she was the first to get the call, from a woman in Davis she had become friendly with through working together over the phone. But before she could tell anyone else, Tina got the word from Peachy Importunato at Warner, who heard it from a Columbia rep, who found out as word filtered down the food chain from Dom Castellano, who was checking out, along with Bruce Springsteen, when they heard about the brouhaha and saw the cops arriving at top speed. They hustled in the direction of the disturbance, and by talking to a few of the refugees they were able to put together most of what happened; then they shared a limo to San Francisco without saying goodbye to anyone. Castellano couldn't stop telling the story to everyone he met, and Springsteen wrote a song about it, but it was too late to be included on the new album.

There was no hero's welcome for Fat Mack Foley in Cincinnati. In point of fact, Fat Mack did not go home for a couple of weeks. Instead, he rented a car and drove to Reno, where he gambled and won and gambled and lost and had sex with two hookers at once. Except for the prostitutes, he paid for everything with his company credit card. When the card started to be declined everywhere, he finally went home, but he never went back to work. He didn't quit, and he wasn't fired. He just never returned.

Incredibly, Richie Vinograd spent less than a week in the hospital. Ironically – no, not ironically or coincidentally, maybe just interestingly – he returned to his office at around the same time that Fat Mack was enjoying himself with his two new friends only 160 miles away. Although he recovered completely, Vinograd never once for the rest of his life spoke about the fight, nor any other aspect of Circular Media's final planning meeting. He only needed to use the cane occasionally, but he never gave it up, even after he had fully recovered physically. People around him learned not to speak about the whole incident, even though it became one of the legendary anecdotes of the entertainment business. It was a Random Note in *Rolling Stone*, and was mentioned with almost entirely false details on "Entertainment Tonight" and in *Entertainment Weekly Magazine*.

As years went by, so many people gave first hand blow-by-blow descriptions of what became known as The Finale in the Valley that, if they were all true, the Crystal Conference Room could never have held all of them. In that sense, it had become like Woodstock. The first one.

The Springsteen song, also called "Finale in the Valley," did not get released until three albums later, but by then it had become a favorite among concertgoers, especially his core fans in New Jersey.

Somehow or other, Brian Fallow had reassured the police and gotten them to leave without even filing so much as a report; George tried to imagine what that must have cost. He promised the management of The Velvet Vineyard something that convinced them not to press charges; that was apparently easier than convincing Vinograd not to press charges, but he had in the end accomplished both. No one else's injuries were significant. Arthur Fishbein, who had been playing golf with Steve Abramowitz at the time of the incident, didn't find out that the conference was over until he showed up for dinner at another fancy restaurant and no one else came.

When he finally got to sit down at his desk, George found that, no surprise, his email inbox was choked with more than three hundred new messages. He spent an hour deleting the spam and separating the ones that looked like they could wait until tomorrow, and then took a closer look at the rest. There were emails from every studio rep and even his marketing counterparts at four other video distributors. Suddenly one seemed to jump out at him. He clicked on it.

FROM: BJF
TO: GWB
RE: recap

George. I'd like you to know that I wrote you a note on Tuesday night, after the big show. I'm going to type it here exactly as I wrote it that night, before all the shit hit the fan the next day.

George: I'm sorry about your presentation today. It was my fault that it didn't go well, not yours. I just want you to know that I read your notes, I understand what you were going to say, it makes perfect sense, and I apologize for screwing you up. I'll convey all of this to the entire group when we get home.

What happened last Wednesday doesn't change any of that. I still look forward to working with you, and I still hope that you will remain a part of the team. You are not a sycophant, and, though I may not be easy to work for, that's the type of person I know I need.

Brian

George didn't mention the email to anybody else at work. He forwarded it to Alice May's email at home, and he spent the rest of the day trying to get caught up.

Arthur Fishbein fired Brian Fallow three weeks later. Along with several pages worth of additional benefits in his severance agreement, he left the company with $2,800,000.

STACY GOT A NEW JOB TWO WEEKS LATER. SHE offered to give George a month's notice, but George thanked her and said that it would be ok if she left right away. The four women who worked under her were subsequently fired, by phone, by someone no one had ever heard of. Ellen Cubbage started to take her freelance side business seriously, and her husband got a promotion, so she was soon able to leave as well.

Hock quit, but he returned a week later, after Staples pleaded with him to stay on as a consultant for the rest of the year until his people could get a grip on what he had lately found out were the unique difficulties and intricacies of video buying. Hock agreed, and he made more money in the last quarter of the year than he had made in salary in the previous sixteen months. Even so, he refused to get on a plane and go to

California so Staples and his team could have hands-on training. They teleconferenced.

Lydia retired, which was what she had wanted to do all along anyway. A dismissal letter came for her the next day, and nobody forwarded it or ever mentioned it to her. She hadn't needed to work for the last several years, and had only kept doing it because she had loved the place and enjoyed all the tumult. After the takeover, the new type of tumult was not in the least enjoyable. Her only real regret was that she had gone to the final Circular planning meeting at all, had not told them to go fuck themselves the day she was "invited."

Groucho and George left on the same day. Groucho had been taking classes for the last five years with people ten to twenty years younger than her, and now she had only one more to go before she could open her own dental practice again. George emailed his two-weeks notice to Angela Crofut in HR. He had been searching for a teaching job, but, unlike when he had begun his career, high school English teachers were no longer in high demand. After a long talk with Alice May, he switched gears.

"We don't need the money," she said. It was true: Will was finishing college, and Sally, who would be starting soon, was already provided for, her tuition, like Will's, securely invested. "You don't have to work right now." When the conversation had started he'd deemed the notion ludicrous. An hour later, it made perfect sense.

George could help Sally with her college applications, she told him. He could keep house and he could get a well-deserved break. Unlike his colleagues who had been pessimistically stressed out for months before the end came, George had forestalled most of that dread, most of that anticipation of the executioner's axe. Then, almost half-a-year's worth of anxiety exploded on him all at once the day after he returned from California.

But now it could all be brushed aside. Although that was easier said than done, it was true. Maybe he'd enroll in graduate school and get a Master's, something he'd never considered before. Then, who knew, maybe teach college, be an adjunct at Rutgers or Drew or Kean.

"Maybe you could write a memoir," Alice May offered brightly.

"Never," George said.

Alice May wouldn't retire next year as they had talked about, and she was relieved because she had dreaded the idea and couldn't figure out why she had even considered it.

By this time, there was only a skeleton crew in Jersey City. The warehouse was no longer used, and where more than a hundred employees had been constantly busy only six months earlier, twenty-two mainly dispirited people remained, pouring through the classifieds, working on their resumes, scaling and catching Frisbees and waiting for the final axe to fall.

In February, Circular sold the building, laid off more than half of the people still there, and moved the nine remaining people to a small suite of offices they'd rented in Hoboken. Those still there were three telemarketers, Andy the long-haired computer guy, Amelia the receptionist, Terry Lunceford, Dave Killian, and Annabelle from the warehouse, who did the filing. She brought her flamboyant, gender-bending ways to filing and typing as she had done with sorting and filling out UPS manifests before, although there was a quieter, sadder tone. Only Killian never changed his style even one little bit, stalking back and forth behind his desk, rarely sitting down, raving into his phone headset. Terry Lunceford's mother, son, brother, and second job assured her that she still had little time to look for anything else. She would stay until the final end, and then get some more hours at the Ultimate, and then find something new.

Killian had posited the notion that, whether she and some of the others came to work every day or not, as long as they never drew attention to themselves, HR might continue to direct deposit their paychecks for the foreseeable future, or at least until the end of the fiscal year. He was always saying things like that. He would have said something very different if had known that, on the same day that Circular Media signed a rental agreement for that office in Hoboken, Arthur Fishbein and his lawyers were in the United States District Court on Pine Street in San Francisco, beginning the complicated process of filing for Chapter Eleven bankruptcy protection for Circular Media. Even Killian hadn't seen it coming.

He should have. Everybody should have.

There was an impenetrable firewall between Fishbein's personal assets and his company. Financing the purchase of Stellar Video, then stopping Stellar from being Stellar, was more than Circular could absorb.

Soon it was springtime, when the tiny grape-berries were blossoming all over the vineyards of Napa Valley. Shopkeepers at florists and plant stores all over Jersey City were dragging wooden shelves and palettes out onto the sidewalks of Communipaw Avenue and Kennedy Boulevard and Grove Street so that the pots of alstromeria, geraniums, daffodils and hyacinths could soak up the sunlight and the commuters passing by could take the hint and pick one up on the way home. By May, the only employees left on the books of Circular Media were Angela Crofut and Richie Vinograd. Angela was in charge of laying off everyone who still remained; Richie was responsible for the auction of every physical asset that could be dumped. On behalf of the record labels and video manufacturers, the bankruptcy creditors' committee had a private security firm on hand at every warehouse location from Davis, CA to Minneapolis to make sure that the $20-30 million worth of unpaid-for inventory remained right where it was. They carried sidearms. But Richie was free to auction off desks, chairs, paper clips, slide projectors and computers. Every single computer was adorned with a cheerful green oval sticker with the words *Y2K compatible!*

Lane Coutell returned to western Massachusetts when it became clear that there was nothing for him to do at the new little office in Hoboken, and he was no longer anybody's boss. He called his girlfriend Kristy to say goodbye, and then he took his wife and kids back to Stockbridge. The branch there had been emptied and shuttered, and Danny and the Juniors were all scattered and gone.

As they passed Exit 18 on the New York State Thruway, he began to hum a tune and drum his fingers lightly on the steering wheel. He sang softly to himself, so as not to wake Judy, his wife, who was sleeping beside him, happily dreaming of their return to the Berkshire town she loved.

> *Laa, la LA la LA la LA!*
> *Laa, la LA la LA la LA!*
> *Come on baby, don't fear the Reaper!*
> *Come and take my hand, don't fear the Reaper!* [1]

Epilogue

Dec. 31,
1999

FADE IN:

INT. - TAVERN - NIGHT

The dimly lit back room of a bar. From the
front room come occasional bursts of
laughter or argument. Back here, a TV set
hanging from the ceiling plays an old black
and white movie silently, the word MUTE
superimposed on the screen. Maybe it's a
color movie on a black and white TV, no way
to tell.

There is a pool table with no balls, and a
dartboard with only one dart. The only dart
is being flung at the board by GEORGE
BECKER, who glances toward the door of the
room before each throw. It's too dark back
here to see whether the dart hit the
dartboard, but we track forward with GEORGE
who strides directly toward it, and we see

him remove the dart, which is an inch off-center from the target's bull's-eye. Then he goes back to the throwing spot, takes a sip from a glass of beer, glances once more at the door, and hurls the dart again, repeating the process in such a manner that we can guess he's been doing this for a while now.

GEORGE checks his watch, looks up at the TV, takes another sip of his beer.

He hesitates, unsure whether to keep playing the mindless dart-solitaire a while longer or leave. He picks up his coat from the back of a chair; just then a WOMAN walks into the back room.

She's wearing a parka with a hood trimmed in fake fur. We can't see her face.

> WOMAN
> I knew you'd be here. I
> wasn't sure about any of the
> others.

> GEORGE
> And here I expected more to
> show. Apparently it's just
> you and me.

The WOMAN removes the hood of her parka. We see that it is ELLEN CUBBAGE.

> CUBBAGE
> I'm sorry I'm so late. I
> thought that I would miss
> you, and then I wouldn't

                    CUBBAGE (continues)
          really know if you had been
          here or not.

GEORGE steps forward to greet her. They hug.

                    GEORGE
          You just caught me. I was
          about to leave.

                    CUBBAGE
          Look. I have it.

She pulls a large manila envelope from
inside her parka. Glinting light shows us
that it has several stamps and different
mailing labels on it, and has been repaired
with tape. We can't make out the addresses.

                    GEORGE
          He mailed it to you! Return
          address...?

                    CUBBAGE
          None. At least not on the
          outside. I haven't opened it.
          But I'll bet we won't find
          anything on the inside
          either, except everything
          that originally went in.

                    GEORGE
          Well, it's late. I've got to
          get home. We're going to some
          godawful millennium party. I
          guess there's only one thing
          left to do. Right?

> CUBBAGE

I guess so.
> (pause, both are silent)

You think you won, don't you?

> GEORGE

Not a chance. Oh for seven.
> (pause. Then)

You won, didn't you?

> CUBBAGE

Au contraire, mon frere. It
cannot be me.

> GEORGE

You had to have done better
than I did.

> CUBBAGE

You're going to find this
hard to believe, but all my
guesses were sarcastic
snarks.

> GEORGE

No. Really?

> CUBBAGE

It's true.

> GEORGE

You were pretty cavalier with
your fifty dollar investment,
weren't you?

> CUBBAGE

Story of my life. But, hey, I
gotta be me. Or something.

They pull chairs up to a table. CUBBAGE
unceremoniously tears the envelope and dumps
the contents on the table between them.
There is indeed no message inside, nothing
but cash and the business cards. She removes
a rubber band from the seven business cards
and examines each one.

          CUBBAGE
      (Reading the first one.)
  No. Nope.
      (Picking up the next one.)

  What? Oh, please, no.
      (Continuing similarly
      through the rest.)

  Wrong.
  Stupid and wrong.
  El-Wrongo.
  Duh.
  Not one even came close. Do
  you want to see them?

          GEORGE
  Absolutely not. I trust your
  judgement.

          CUBBAGE
  You always did.
      (pause)

  You usually did.

          GEORGE
  And I especially don't want
  to see mine. I don't need one
  more reminder of how naïve I
  was when I thought I was my
  most sophisticated.

There is a long pause while the two of them remain facing each other. The quiet moment is broken by rowdy drunken singing from the front bar.

> GEORGE
> What— Whaddya think we should do with the money? We can't even send it back to everybody. Not everybody is reachable.

> CUBBAGE
> We agreed that the winner had to be present to collect.

> GEORGE
> (surprised)
> We did?

> CUBBAGE
> No, we didn't. I just made that up. But unless you have a better suggestion…
> > (She waits to see if he does. He doesn't.)
> > (In an officious voice)
>
> Now, by the powers that have not been vested in me, I nevertheless pronounce the contest tied, the winnings split, and the pact over.

> GEORGE
> Sounds about right to me.

She picks up the cash and peels off two fifties, one twenty, four tens and three fives, placing them in front of GEORGE.)

>   CUBBAGE
>   Take it.

When he does, she pockets her half. Then she sweeps the little white cards back into the envelope.

>   Do you want them? No?

CUBBAGE folds the envelope into a small square, looks around, locates a trash can and tosses it in.

>   CUBBAGE
>   Well, it's been very nice to
>   see you.

>   GEORGE
>   And you as well.

>   CUBBAGE
>   It's nearly Y2K. Do you think
>   the world's gonna blow up or
>   planes are gonna fall out of
>   the sky in a couple of hours?

>   GEORGE
>   No. I think that was just one
>   more unnecessary panic.

>   CUBBAGE
>   And not even a fun one. Give
>   my regards to Alice May and
>   your kids.

>   GEORGE
>   I will. Say hello to Jack for
>   me. Is he doing any-

                    CUBBAGE
No, not really. Hey, I
finally read Alice May's
book. Impressive. All those
years when I saw you fiddling
with little pieces of string,
I thought you were cracking
up. But that wasn't it at
all, was it?

                    GEORGE
Nope.

                    CUBBAGE
Bet they were shopping lists!
"Honey, don't forget to bring
home a quart of milk…"

                    GEORGE
Sometimes. More often they
were love notes.

                    CUBBAGE
Okay, I'll choose to believe
you.

A STRANGER appears. He leans over a jukebox,
perusing his options. It's so gloomy back
here that they can't really see his face.
They hadn't noticed him walk in. It's
possible he'd been sitting there for a
while.

THE STRANGER searches the juke, finds
something he likes. He addresses them.

                    STRANGER
You folks mind?

GEORGE doesn't get what he's asking at
first. Then he does.

> GEORGE
> Go ahead. Knock yourself out.

> CUBBAGE
> We're leaving in a minute
> anyhow.

But the stranger has already inserted his
quarter and left the room.

The jukebox comes on. The record that has
dropped onto the turntable was only recently
released on vinyl and CD. The A side was a
big hit for Bruce Springsteen and the E
Street Band; THE STRANGER has selected the
B-side. It's a call-and-response kind of
duet, featuring Springsteen and his right
hand man, saxophonist, deep bass vocalist
and crowd-favorite, known by his band name
The Big Man, Clarence Clemons.)

> *(BRUCE) Nobody knew what was*
> *goin down in Cali*
> *(CLARENCE) Somebody said it*
> *was*
> *A football rally*
> *(BRUCE) What? No way. More*
> *like*
> *A catfight in an alley*
> *(BRUCE) Turns out everybody*
> *was wrong*
> *(CLARENCE) Why the hell'd it*
> *take 'em so long?*
> *(BRUCE AND CLARENCE TOGETHER)*
> *Jump back, look around for*
> *Susie and Sally*

> *Windows breakin ground is*
> *shakin*
> *(BRUCE) Earthquakes always*
> *happen in Cali*
> *(CLARENCE) Not this time son*
> *-*
>
> *It's the* **Finale in the Valley**[7]

CUBBAGE and GEORGE look at each other in amazement. They laugh.

> CUBBAGE
> Not irony! Um… Just
> coincidence.

> GEORGE
> Pretty fucking ironic
> coincidence.
>   (pause)
>
> Wait. Who… Who played it?

They look all around the back room, then check the bar room in front. Only a few old guys and women are sitting at the bar, and they all look as though they could not have gotten up, walked into the back room and figured out how to operate a jukebox without several cups of black coffee first. GEORGE and CUBBAGE grab their coats and race out the front door.

EXT. - IN FRONT OF THE BAR - NIGHT

They look up and down the street, both sides, all directions. But the street is dead. Had they heard a car peel out and pull away? The eerie coincidence, if that's what it had been, has them rattled. Finally they

give up, and look at each other, both
shrugging.

> GEORGE
> Curiouser and curiouser.

> CUBBAGE
> It couldn't be somebody...

> GEORGE
> Just a coincidence. An
> ironic, eerie fucking
> coincidence.

> CUBBAGE
> Good. Beause I never believed
> in ghosts and I don't feel
> like starting now.

They both shake their heads. They both hug
themselves for warmth.

A quiet moment on the empty street. No cars
nearby, none cruising by either. No people
appear.

Then...

> GEORGE
> Hey, it was fun for a time,
> wasn't it?

> CUBBAGE
> Absolutely. For a
> surprisingly long time,
> actually. I know now that we
> were lucky to have it last as
> long as it did.

> GEORGE
> You're right. And in a way,
> everything is better than
> ever, kind of, for most of
> us. Well, sort of—

> CUBBAGE
> No, it's true. Of course it
> is. Everything only always
> gets better.

With that, she turns on her heel and walks
away. We watch her until she gets to the
corner and turns.

> GEORGE
> Bye! See you!

Without looking back she raises her arm and
waggles her gloved fingers. Then she turns a
corner and disappears. GEORGE turns and, for
a moment, considers his reflection in the
window of the bar. Then he puts his hand up
to the glass, trying to see through the
reflection into the barroom inside. He sees
nothing of note.

He looks up and down the street once more.
Then he too turns, and walks down the
sidewalk in the opposite direction.

FADE OUT.

THE END.

For more information about the books and activities of Richard Goffman, as well as other 99%BOOKS authors including Linda Watkins and Gino Bardi, go to www.richardgoffman.com.

You can email the author at Richard@richardgoffman.com or write via earthly mail to

Richard Goffman
c/o 99%BOOKS
57 Compton Road
Sussex, NJ 07461